Corrupted by a Gangsta

Destiny Skai

Lock Down Publications and
Ca$h Presents

Corrupted by a Gangsta

A Novel by **Destiny Skai**

Destiny Skai

Lock Down Publications
P.O. Box 870494
Mesquite, Tx 75187

Visit our website
www.lockdownpublications.com

Lock Down Publications
Like our page on Facebook: Lock Down Publications @
www.facebook.com/lockdownpublications.ldp
Cover design and layout by: **Dynasty Cover Me**
Book interior design by: **Shawn Walker**
Edited by: **Lauren Burton**

4

Stay Connected with Us!

Text **LOCKDOWN** to 22828 to stay up-to-date with new releases, sneak peaks, contests and more...

Submission Guideline.

Submit the first three chapters of your completed manuscript to ldpsubmissions@gmail.com, subject line: Your book's title. The manuscript must be in a .doc file and sent as an attachment. Document should be in Times New Roman, double spaced and in size 12 font. Also, provide your synopsis and full contact information. If sending multiple submissions, they must each be in a separate email.

Have a story but no way to send it electronically? You can still submit to LDP/Ca$h Presents. Send in the first three chapters, written or typed, of your completed manuscript to:

LDP: Submissions Dept
Po Box 870494
Mesquite, Tx 75187

DO NOT send original manuscript. Must be a duplicate.

Provide your synopsis and a cover letter containing your full contact information.

Thanks for considering LDP and Ca$h Presents.

Corrupted by a Gangsta

ACKNOWLEDGEMENTS

I would like to thank all of my readers for rocking with me throughout my literary journey and the new ones that have recently come aboard. The love and support is surreal and greatly appreciated. I can honestly say that this is the best series that I have penned to date, with word of mouth it's guaranteed to be a classic and there will be many more in the future.

If this is your first time reading my work please go and check out The Fetti Girls and Bride of a Hustla, which is available on Amazon. My first series Bride of a Hustla has a movie, so if you would like to purchase it visit my website: www.thadspot.com.

Upon finishing this book, please be sure to leave a review. They are important to me being that it will help me grow as an author. From the bottom of my heart I appreciate the love and support from all of you.

~Love Destiny

Destiny Skai

Prologue

District Attorney Derrick Jacobs paced the floor slowly with both hands in his pockets, while preparing to deliver the closing argument for the prosecution. The jurors' eyes followed him with anticipation. Some wore nervous smiles, while the others sat with their mouths wide open.

"Ladies and gentlemen of the court, I would like to start off by saying thank you for your time, patience and sacrifices that you have made to ensure that justice will be served today."

He walked over and placed two hands on the jurors' box and looked each man and woman in their eyes. "You have the power today to make sure this young girl gets the justice and safety she deserves." Pointing in the section where Zuri was sitting, he continued. "Unfortunately, Zuri Monroe missed out on her childhood and doing the things that little girls do. But, you can make sure that she can start the healing process and enjoy the rest of her teenage years and adult life, by convicting the pedophile that took away her innocence."

Mr. Jacobs took a few steps back and turned to face the defendant. "You saw the evidence and you saw the most painful, yet emotional testimony from the victim's twelve-year-old sister, about what she saw her father doing to her older sister." Placing his pointer finger to his temple, he glanced over to the jury. "Imagine how you would feel walking into the room and witnessing such a heinous act." Pausing, he stood in the middle of the floor, staring Daman down like he was the lowest, most disgusting scum of the earth, while pointing at him. He picked up where he left off, "Being committed by your very own father. The one man who is supposed to love and protect you from sick and twisted individuals like himself."

Daman returned a hard, cold evil glare at Mr. Jacobs, not blinking once. In his mind, he said to himself, *Who the fuck this Uncle Tom ass nigga think he is, talking down on me like I'm a fuckin' rapist and shit? He lucky I ain't out on bond, 'cause I'll tie his bitch ass up and make him watch me fuck the shit out his daughter and his wife. I ain't no fuckin' pedophile. I love my daughter and I would never let anyone hurt her.* Daman grinned deviously at his idea and grabbed his stiffening crotch.

"At ten years old, little girls should be playing with baby dolls, not their vaginas or male genitals. He manipulated his daughter, making her think that what they were doing was okay. She trusted him and he betrayed her by doing despicable acts to her."

Mr. Jacobs walked over to the table and picked up a poster-size photo of Zuri when she was ten years old and held it up for the jury to see. "Look at this photo of this sweet and innocent child. Now, look at the monster, who was thirty-four years old when it all began. We can all add in here. That's an age difference of twenty-four years. I want each and every last one of you to close your eyes and visualize the pain this child went through on a daily basis, being constantly raped by her father. This is Zuri's story. This little girl was playing at home when her father decided she was old enough to fulfill his needs. He engaged her in performing oral sex on him for years, until her thirteenth birthday. Daman waited until his youngest daughter went to bed to creep into Zuri's bedroom, rip off her pajamas and panties. Then, he climbed on top of her, penetrating her tiny vagina with painful thrusts, until she bled out all over the bed."

His voice began to crack, as he went into details so vivid and deep that he started to tear up, thinking about the same chain of events that happened to his sister. The only difference was, his sister was murdered afterwards. "She was an innocent child," he shouted. "A baby. You tore into her flesh and made her suffer at your deceitful hands, over and over again. That's not love." Tears rolled down his face. Quickly grabbing a handkerchief, he dabbed his eyes and focused on the jury. "I apologize for my emotions, but this case is heartbreaking and it upsets me that a father could do that his very own daughter."

Mr. Jacobs regained his composure and continued. "That abuse continued for three more years, until the youngest sister walked in while he was raping her and called the police. That little girl heard her sister's muffled cries and knew something was wrong, so she called for help. She saved her sister's life and now, it's your turn to do the same and find Daman Monroe guilty on all charges. Zuri deserves justice. Zuri deserves peace."

Destiny Skai

Chapter 1

Zuri

Darkness managed to catch me after leaving my bikini wax appointment, so I scurried through the parking lot to get to my car. It was already cold outside, so I was trying to get to my heater. Florida had the weirdest weather. A little under two months ago, on Christmas Day, it was barely cool and now that we were in February, the ground hog has seen his shadow. Now, we would endure some cold weather for another six weeks, but I wasn't complaining. That meant I could take advantage of wearing my boots a little bit longer.

The lot was damn near vacant, so it had me a little nervous. Plus, the crickets' sounds were annoying my soul, making me feel like I was on the scene of a sick and twisted horror movie. Once I was close to my car, I clicked the locks on my Infiniti Q50, jumped inside, tossed my bag onto the passenger seat and started up the engine right away. Taking a deep breath and blowing it into my hands, I laughed at my paranoia and turned on the heater.

"Zuri, get a grip."

My nerves were shot for no reason, so I popped the top and took a shot straight from the bottle. The alcohol was cold, since Javier, the owner and friend of mine, had just taken it from the freezer.

"Woo!" I licked my top lip where the liquor made me a little mustache. "That was good. I'm getting fucked up tonight." Before I put the bottle up, I took two more shots and pulled out the parking lot and onto Northeast 26th Street.

It was a Thursday night and I was ready to go home and unwind. I was off that Friday, so I was about to enjoy a three-day weekend. My job as a counselor with Kids in Distress could be very stressful at times, but nonetheless I loved what I did. In my heart, I had a strong passion for helping children that suffered from abuse, being that I was one myself. The only difference was, I enjoyed it. As I made a left onto Andrews Avenue, my phone started to ring, so I answered it on Bluetooth.

"Hello."

"Hey, baby. What's going on?" Daman's voice boomed through the speakers.

"Just getting off work." His voice always made me smile.

"This late? Where you going now?" he questioned.

"I'm on my way home."

"What'chu got on?"

"Some fitted jeans that hug me in all the right places and your favorite boy shorts."

"Mm. That sounds good right now."

"And, so do you. I have some Hennessy, so I'm ready for whatever tonight."

"On video?"

The thought of seeing his pretty dick on camera made me hungry for him. "Of course. That's how I prefer it. I need you to see my fresh Brazilian wax."

"You did that for me?" His voice was low and deep. I could just melt right now.

"Of course I did. I can't wait for you to come home, 'cause it's so lonely without you."

"I feel the same way. I'm sick of being around niggas, day in and day out. This shit will drive you crazy."

"I can only imagine, but that's what I'm here for. To make your time easy."

"My dick so hard right now, thinkin' 'bout you and the way you used to ride it." The way he was grunting told me he got started already. "I can feel your lips gripping it."

"I'm almost home." I sighed. "You making me so horny right now. I can't pay attention to the road."

"Pull over."

"Okay." The light had just turned yellow, so I hit the gas to make sure I caught it. Making a left onto 15th, I drove one block before I turned off and parked in front of a warehouse.

"I'm ready." Before I did anything, I made sure my doors were locked. Then, I reached over for the bottle and took a long swig.

"Hold on."

"Okay." There was some rustling, then some talking, but I couldn't make out what was being said. Then, there was more rustling. "Hello."

"Yeah."

"This some bullshit."

"What happened?" He had me curious.

"They about to lock us down for the night. These dumb ass niggas in here fighting and shit."

Daman was disappointed and I could hear it in his voice. As bad as he needed it, so did I, because it had been a while since I had sex with someone and I was tired of using my bullets and vibrators. My body needed a human with a heartbeat, like ASAP.

"We gone have to hold off until tomorrow. They gone be in here soon."

"That sucks. You had me turned on for nothing."

"I know. Shit, I feel the same way."

Daman had been locked up for six years and he expected me to close down shop until he came home. As bad as I wanted to, that just wasn't possible. My sexual desires had always been high since I was ten years old. That was the age I started masturbating. I became curious when I saw my older brother having sex with a girl in the house when we were home alone. The noises she was making didn't sound like she was in pain and it looked like she was enjoying it. Once I saw that, I started hiding in his closet, so I could watch him in action. From there, I started to touch myself and take longer baths. I would sit in the bathtub and let the water run between my legs. That made me feel good for a while, but I wanted more. Sadly, I didn't lose my virginity until I was thirteen and Daman was the one to break me in.

"Don't worry. I'll be over here patiently waiting as usual." I breathed heavily into the phone.

"You better be. I trained you and you belong to me." There was so much authority in his voice, it sent tingles up and down my spine. That aggressive shit turned me on.

"Damn, I wish I could stay on the phone with you, but I gotta go. I'll call you tomorrow."

"Okay."

"I love you."

"I love you too."

The phone hung up and I leaned my head back against the headrest. My body was tense and heavily aroused, but my heart was hurting. Tears made themselves present and rolled down my cheeks. I was madly in love with Daman and I wanted to be with him, but he still had three more years to do. To me, that felt like an eternity, but I knew he was worth the wait. In all the years he had been gone, I

16

never met a man that possessed his dominant qualities or similarities. Often, I found myself looking, but no one I dealt with came close. These new-age dudes were too soft for me. I was hardheaded and I liked to talk back, so I needed someone a little more challenging and stern to live up to my expectations. Sometimes, I wanted to be told what to do, similar to a father-figure. It was my sister's fault that Daman was in prison in the first place. If she would've never caught us having sex and called the police, he would still be here. That dreadful day played in my head all the time.

"Next year, you'll be eighteen and no one can do nothing about our relationship. We can move to New Jersey and start over, since there is no penalty there."

A huge smile spread across my lips, while Daman was on top thrusting in and out of me. I wrapped my legs around his waist and pulled his face close to mine. Our lips touched and I slipped my tongue into his mouth and kissed him hard. That was the best news I heard all day. Daman grabbed one of my legs, placed it on his shoulder and went deep, causing me to moan loudly.

"Shh." He placed his hand over my mouth and pounded away at my pelvis. My sounds were now muffled, to keep me from being so loud. But, no one could've prepared me for what was about to happen next. The door flew open and hit the wall hard.

Boom!

Daman and I both froze.

"Ooh, I'm telling," my little sister shouted before running out the room.

Both of us jumped up and tried to catch her. I grabbed the sheet and wrapped myself up in it, while Daman slipped on his pants. We both took off down the hallway and by the time we hit the living room, she had the phone to her ear.

"My daddy is on top of my sister with no clothes on. I just saw them."

That was the worst day of my life. Our father was arrested and Mehzani and I were sent to live with our aunt, Daman's sister, to keep us from going to foster care. It was cool in the beginning, until the trial came and I wouldn't testify against him. That evil bitch had me placed in foster care because she said I was a sick child and I needed help if I thought having sex with my father was okay.

The sound of police sirens brought me back to reality, causing me to jump out my skin. To the left of me, I counted six police cars flying in one direction.

"What the hell going on around here?" All the excitement had my attention. "Let me take my ass in the house."

Seconds later, my passenger window came crashing in. When I looked over, some guy was sticking his hand through the window and opening up my door, so I screamed and tried to jump out the car. He jammed the gun into my side.

"Shut the fuck up and sit'cho yo ass down. You ain't goin' nowhere," he demanded, while placing a black duffle bag on the floor between his feet.

The minute I felt that gun, I knew to be quiet because he looked like he wouldn't hesitate to pull the trigger. I placed both hands on the steering wheel and took a deep breath to calm my nerves. Then, I looked him in the eyes, so I could get a good look at his face. "I will take you wherever you want go, just don't hurt me."

He licked his lips and his face softened just a little bit, revealing a dimple. "Damn, you a pretty muthafucka. Believe me, ma. I don't wanna hurt you but if I have to, I will."

He stroked my chin with his finger. "Just don't do no stupid shit and I won't blow this pretty-ass face away."

"Okay." My eyes stayed on him while nodding my head up and down. "I won't, I promise."

"That's all I needed to hear, beautiful. Just relax and do the speed limit. The minute you drive crazy and get us pulled, just remember that I ain't got shit to lose and I'll splatter your brain all over this muthafucka."

"You're safe with me."

"Good. These crackas don't need help doing their muthafuckin' job no way. Your job as a queen is to help to the black man, whether he's right or wrong in this crooked-ass, white man's world."

My handsome captor grabbed his side and frowned. It looked as if he was in pain. That's when I noticed there was blood on his shirt. "Do you want to go to the hospital?"

"No hospitals."

After he objected, I pulled out and headed east towards Federal Highway. I lived in Victoria Park, which was right down the street and I wanted him out of my vehicle fast as fuck. Every now and again, I would stare at him to see what he was doing. Each time, he was checking the wound on his stomach. Sweat was dripping down his face, so I turned off the heater.

"You don't look so well, you sure you don't want me to take you to the hospital?"

"No," he snapped. "Just do what I say and hook a right up here on the next street."

"I have some napkins in the glovebox. You may want to clean your face."

I did as I was told and followed his directions. He did the same. My inquisitive mind wanted to know what the hell he did and why was he running. He was too saucy to be out here doing stickups in expensive threads and high-priced jewelry. The way this mouth was set up, I knew I needed to keep quiet so I wouldn't set him off.

"Make a left." Just as I hit the corner, red, white and blue lights were everywhere. "Fuck!" he shouted.

We ran right into a fuckin' roadblock. There were police officers everywhere and I already knew they were looking for my passenger.

"You want me to turn around?" My voice was shaky.

"No!" The bass in his voice caused me to jump. "Just keep going so we don't bring any suspicions to this car."

"Got it. Calm down and zip up your jacket." I would hate to see his fine ass go to prison. That would be a waste of a fine piece of specimen and in my opinion prison was no place for a black man. All they needed was some guidance and a woman to hold them down the right way.

"Beautiful, remember what I said." He touched my face again and this time it sent a tingle down my spine and up my vagina. A bitch's pussy was drippin' in these jeans. *Lawd, I needed some dick bad!*

"I have nothing to lose and the only way ya family gon' recognize you is through ya dental records. You understand me?" I nodded my head *yes*.

He pulled open my glovebox and took out my registration. "Zuri Monroe. So, you live at five-twenty-five North Victoria Park Road." After he read my info out loud, he took a picture of it. He put my document back, hid the gun underneath the seat and tossed the bag into the backseat.

By the time we got to the group of officers, he was laid back in the seat like he was sleep. The officer walked up and shined his flashlight into the car.

"Good evening, ma'am. How are you?"

"I'm fine. Thanks for asking. What's going on?"

"There was a robbery in the neighborhood and a shooting. Do you live around here?"

"Yes." I glanced over at my captor. "Me and my husband live right around the corner."

"Okay. I need to see your license. We're only letting you through if you're a resident."

I grabbed my purse from the back seat to retrieve my wallet. After a little digging, I handed it to him. "Here you go."

"Thanks." He shined the light on my picture and handed it back. "What happened to your window?"

His question caught me off guard, but I had to be quick on my toes. "Some kids were throwing rocks and shattered it."

"You need to hurry up and get that fixed. That tint will only hold the glass for so long."

"Yes. I'm getting it fixed tomorrow."

"Excuse me, sir, could you look up for a moment please?"

"He's tired from driving trucks for weeks at a time." I placed my hand on his shoulder and shook him. "Bae, look up for a moment. It's a roadblock."

Slowly moving his head, he raised it high enough to make very little eye contact with the officer. "What's going on, Officer?"

When I looked back up at the officer, he had his hand on his holster this time. "We're looking for a robbery suspect."

"Oh, well I hope y'all catch him." He laid back down and closed his eyes.

"Yep, I think we just did." The officer pulled his gun from his holster and aimed it. "Freeze."

My heart dropped to the pit of my stomach and I was afraid of what was about to happen next. If my captor even thought I tipped him off a little bit, I was in trouble. Three officers took off running and the officer at my window looked at me. "You're free to go and go straight home until we have apprehended the suspect."

My ass was confused and relieved at the same time when he ran off. My head swiveled in their direction and I saw another black male standing on the sidewalk with his hands up, talking to the police. That was my cue to pull off.

"Where am I taking you?" I asked.

"You heard the police." He sat up. "We going to five-twenty-five North Victoria Park Road."

That was definitely not a part of the plan, but at that moment, I was out of any other options. In less than two minutes, I was pulling up into my driveway.

"Pull the car into the garage," my captor insisted.

"Why?" I frowned.

"Your window is busted." He shrugged his shoulders. "I mean, unless you want something to get inside, like rain and mess up your car."

"Oh yeah," I replied sarcastically and rolled my eyes. "I forgot you knocked my window out."

"I saw that."

"I didn't hide it."

"Don't worry about the window, bae. I'ma give you the money to get it fixed."

"Good." I smiled at the name he called me and hit the remote on the sun visor and the garage door eased open at a slow pace. I pulled inside and hit the button once again to close it.

"Get your things and come on." It took a minute for me to grab my things and open the door.

My captor grabbed his things and got out the car like he belonged in my home. All I could do was hope he was a man of character, and upheld his end of the deal by not hurting me.

Destiny Skai

Chapter 2

Brick

Zuri was the baddest chick I had seen in a while. She had this flawless, smooth brown sugar skin, brown eyes and dimples. Her hair was jet black and it stopped at the middle of her back. As I walked behind her, she escorted me through the garage and into the kitchen. My eyes were like an infrared beam on her ass. It wasn't huge, but it was the right size for her shape. When she walked, her hips swished from side to side. That made me wonder if she was doing that on purpose. Too bad we didn't meet on better terms, 'cause I would've snatched shorty up real quick.

"Would you like something to drink?" She looked back at me with a slight smile on her face.

"Sure." We both paused at the refrigerator. She opened the door and I peeped inside. "I'll take a bottled water."

"Here you go."

"Thanks."

The kitchen was dope as fuck. It was all-white, with Calcutta white and gold marble countertops, and forest green appliances. Based on the set-up and all-white décor, I knew she didn't have any kids. If she did, they had to be grown and she wasn't as young as I thought she was.

"You can have a seat at the table right there." She pointed towards the dining room area next to the kitchen. "I have a first-aid kit in the bathroom that I need to grab."

Zuri walked towards me and placed her bags on the table. My expression had to be worth a thousand words or she was psychic, by the way she stared me down.

"The bathroom is right through this door. Don't worry. I won't do anything to set you off. I'm only trying to help."

After that explanation, I couldn't say shit, but nod my head and take a seat. My gun was stored away in the duffle bag. Something told me I didn't have anything to worry about. Shorty seemed sincere with the help and I'm normally a good judge of character. Zuri came back quick with a first-aid kit in her hand. She sat it down on the table, along with a box of latex gloves and a plastic bag.

"Take off your shirt and put it in that bag." While she set up the area and put on the gloves, I stood up and followed her simple instructions. The wound on my stomach wasn't too painful, but it didn't feel good either, as I pulled the fabric that had dried against my bloody skin. To keep my mind off of it, I whistled until it was off completely.

"Are you..." Zuri paused and her mouth was agape. Her eyes were dreamy, but she wasn't giving me any type of eye contact. They were more so on my chest and torso. There was something about these South Florida women and men that wore gray sweats. It was amusing, 'cause my package definitely fit the bill.

"I work out a lot." I laughed.

My six-pack, firm chest and broad shoulders were the result of a five-year-bid in the feds. My skin was rich and smooth like chocolate, 'cause I took pride in my body and health. The waves on my head were deep enough to drown every bitch in South Florida and just like Zuri, I had a dimple. Shorty was definitely intrigued by the six-foot stranger that stood in her kitchen. Body language was a muthafucka, so I knew she no longer saw me as a threat, but a treat instead.

"Um. No." She sighed and giggled nervously. "That's not what I was going to say. I was about to ask if you wanted a shot to take your mind off the pain."

"Wha'chu got? I don't like that fruity shit."

"Hennessy," she replied.

"Oh, so you like it rough, huh?" The hesitation in her voice clarified three things for me. Indeed, beautiful liked it rough and she was feelin' the king, but I was making her uncomfortable under these circumstances.

"No. I just prefer my liquor to be dark."

Her response made me lick my lips to prepare for my slick comment, but her phone started ringing. She looked at me for approval.

"Who calling you this time of night?" I asked out of curiosity.

"Probably my neighbor. He checks on me at night to make sure I made it inside."

"You sure that ain't ya boyfriend?"

"I don't have a boyfriend." She answered that rather quickly, so yeah, she wanted me.

"Let it ring."

"If I don't answer, he's going to come over." Her voice was soft, like a child trying to get their way.

"He won't think you home if your car is in the garage."

"Oh, right. I forgot about that." She walked over to the dishwasher and pulled out two glasses. "Do you want ice with that?"

"Nah." She came back to the table and fixed me a double shot. I downed it in one gulp. "Fix me another one." I downed that one too. "I'm ready."

"Lay on the bench, so I can get you cleaned up."

"A'ight."

Zuri placed the towel at my side. "Hold this and don't move." I could feel her hands on my side. "No matter what you feel, don't move."

A cold liquid hit my skin and burned me immediately and I hollered. "What the hell is that?"

"It's rubbing alcohol. I have to disinfect the area, so hold still." She poured it on again and I screamed like a bitch. That shit had me breathing like I was in labor. Zuri was laughing. "Are you serious right now?"

"Hell, yeah. That shit burns."

Zuri took ten minutes to clean me up and patch me up decent. She stood over me and reached for my hand. "Come on. You'll live. It's just a flesh wound."

"You a nurse or some shit?"

"No, I'm not a nurse, but I used to be a medical assistant."

"Thank you." She held my hand, as I sat up in place. "I appreciate your help and not turning me in."

"You're welcome." She sat down in the chair across from me. "So, you want to tell me your name and why you busted my window?"

"Not really."

She folded her arms across her chest. "That's the least you can do for holding me hostage."

My thought process was fucked up at this moment and I was so captivated by her beauty, I went ahead and gave her some small details. "This dude owed me some cash, so I stepped to him. Shit got out of hand and bullets started to fly, so I took what belonged to me and took off. That's how I got shot."

"And, what's your name?" She wasn't letting that go.

"They call me Brick."

"Oh, yeah?"

"Yep." There was a knock on the door, so I took my ratchet from my duffle bag. "Who is that?"

"I don't know."

"Who are you expecting?" I cocked my bitch back, prepared to bust her pretty ass open to the white meat.

She panicked when she saw that heat. "I swear, I'm not expecting anybody. It's probably my neighbor. I told you he checks on me."

"Stand up." I grabbed my jacket from the table and put it on. "Get rid of whoever it is at the door, or there will be brain matter all over this bitch." My tone was hard when I spoke to her through gritted teeth. She needed to know I wasn't no muthafuckin' joke.

Zuri walked through the foyer and I made sure to stay close on her heels. I didn't know what shorty's profession was, but she was living large in this bitch. The living room had high-vaulted ceilings, a nice ass fireplace with a big screen TV hanging above it, a platinum rug, soft gray plush sofas and a chrome and glass center table. Needless to say, I was impressed with her impeccable taste. She approached the French doors, so I stood off to the side closest to the hallway with my gun at my side. Zuri looked at me, awaiting my signal for her to open the door. I nodded my head.

"Who is it?"

"It's Jerry."

Zuri unlocked the door and cracked it just a little. "Hey, Jerry. What's going?"

"I just came by to check on you since I called and you didn't answer."

"Oh, my phone must be on vibrate still. I'm okay though, thanks for stopping by."

"The police are in the area going door to door, looking for a suspect involved in a robbery and shooting."

"I ran into the road block on my way home and I saw them arresting someone. So, I believe they got who they're looking for."

"Oh okay. Where's your car?"

"It's in the garage."

This Jerry cat was working my last nerve and if he didn't leave, I was gone peel his muthafuckin' cap back. Zuri better get rid of him fast and I meant in the next ten seconds. I waved my gun in her direction to get her attention. She glanced over quickly and looked back at Jerry.

"Okay, well again thanks for checking on me, but I'm about to wind down and relax. Goodnight."

Zuri tried to close the door, but he stopped her. "Wait. You don't want any company?"

"N-no, that's not a good idea," she stumbled over her words.

It was time to put an end to all of this. So, I walked towards the door. "What's going on, baby? Who at the door?"

When I stepped behind Zuri, I grabbed her around the waist, right at her bikini line, and pulled her close to me so she could feel the gun tucked away in my waistband. Jerry's eyes stretched wide, as he watched me plant a kiss on top of her head.

"Oh, I didn't know you had company. Hi, I'm her neighbor, Jerry." He hit me with that corny, white, rich man laugh. "I came over to tell her about the police patrolling the area." He extended his hand, but I didn't.

"Cleanliness is next to godliness, but I'm Rashawn and it's nice to meet you. Thanks for checking on her, but I'll make sure she's safe from here. Have a good night."

The door slammed, when I pushed it in that cornball's face. Right after that, Zuri made sure the locks were secure. My grip was still tight and I really didn't want her to move because my heavy snake was hard like a rock. Her ass probably thought it was my gun. That was probably why she didn't move my hand just yet. Her scent was tantalizing, like a sweet forbidden fruit. There was nothing like a woman who could be outside and still smell like she was fresh out the shower. For a brief second, I closed my eyes and pictured myself digging in them guts from behind.

Zuri cleared her throat. "We gone stand here all night?"

"Oh, my bad." My hesitation game was strong, but I let her go and followed her back into the kitchen. We sat down and she fixed herself a drink this time.

"You have trust issues, huh?" She was so cute when she rolled her eyes.

Her question caught me off guard, but I was always prepared. "It depends. Why do you ask?"

"I told you I would get rid of whoever was at the door, but you pulled your gun out on me anyway."

"I had to be sure, and I didn't point it directly at you."

"Listen, I don't like the police and if I wanted them involved, you would be in cuffs already. They killing enough of us already, so I wouldn't dare assist them or provide them with the opportunity for target practice."

"I can respect that."

"Good. So, can you please put that thing away?"

I looked at her ass like she was crazy. "You think I should trust you?"

"Why not? I trusted the fact that you wouldn't hurt me and so far, you haven't."

"Zuri." The use of her first name was important, so I made sure I used it. I needed her to see me for who I really was. "I'm not going to hurt you. I promise you that and I know you don't know me, but if I wanted to hurt you, I would've shot you and took your car. All I wanted was a ride out of the fucked-up situation I was in and you did that."

Zuri took a deep breath and gazed into my eyes like she was my woman and we were in love, but trying to fix our problems. "I believe you won't hurt me. I really do. All I want is for you to prove that to me, so I could feel comfortable in my home. Please don't make me feel like a prisoner. I won't go back on my word. I promise."

The sincerity in her words melted my heart and I felt like I could really trust her. So, to show her I was serious and a man of my word, I put the gun away. "It's gone and I won't pull it out until I leave. I just need to sit here until the coast is clear. Is that okay with you?"

"Sure. You already in here." She giggled. "Have a drink while you wait and tell me about yourself."

This girl had to be as crazy as me. She was too damn comfortable being a hostage, but I also believed that God brought people into our lives for a reason. Maybe it was in his plan for me to meet this beautiful woman, so she could save my life. I reached back into the duffle bag, pulled out a stack of neatly wrapped bills and slid it across the table.

"Here, beautiful, this is for your window and hospitality. I don't know where I would be right now if it wasn't for you."

"No. I can't take that from you. So, put that away." She slid it back in front of me.

God, you must be playing with me right now. I never met a woman who turned down five grand in my life.

All I could do was smile on the inside. "It's the least I could do. A nigga would probably be outlined in chalk or in a body bag right now, if you didn't help me get away." I slid the money back over to her, but this time I kept my hand on top of it. "Keep it for me, please."

Zuri placed her hand on top of mine. "If you insist, but you really don't have to do that."

"I want to."

Our eyes locked and we stared at one another for what felt like an eternity. While I was in the feds, I did a lot of reading to elevate my mind and thought process. Studies have shown that by gazing into a stranger's eyes, it helps build passionate feelings towards the opposite sex. And, that's what we were. *Strangers,* but I wanted to change all of that if she gave me the opportunity to do so. At any second, I was expecting her to shy away and break our eye contact, but she didn't. Her focus remained on me.

"So, what do you want to talk about?" she asked.

"I wanna know everything about you and I'll tell you all about me. Do we have a deal?"

"We have a deal." Ma was blushing hard as hell. She was definitely feeling a nigga.

Chapter 3

Zuri

Brick and I sat, talked and laughed like old friends for the past two hours and surprisingly, we had so much in common. This was beyond my wildest imagination. It just wasn't registering that a few hours ago, this man held me captive with a weapon and now, he was in the comfort of my home having drinks. No one would ever believe this story. Shit, I barely believe it. There was something about him that intrigued me from the time he got into my car. I wasn't sure if it was his dominance, swag, or the fact that he's dangerous to a certain degree. Whatever it was, I was feeling it. I giggled to myself. *Maybe it was the alcohol.* The bottle was almost empty, so I fixed me another one and put the rest in his glass.

"You trying to get me drunk?" Brick asked.

"Why not? I am."

"Yeah, I see." He took a sip of his drink and sat his glass down on the table. "Do you believe in the Law of Attraction?"

"Huh?" Now, he had me stumped.

"Law of Attraction," he repeated. My eyes rolled around in my head, but I drew a blank. "It's the belief that if you focus on positive or negative experiences, that's what you bring into your life. It goes the same way with meeting people. I believe we met for a reason."

"And, what would that reason be?"

"I don't know. Maybe it was so you could save my save my life." Brick reached across the table and grabbed my hand. "I'm hoping that I could find out in greater detail."

"Maybe." Everything he said just sounded so sexy to me and I felt like putty in his hands.

"We met for a reason and I'm not in jail for a reason."

"I agree." I downed the last of my drink and stood up. "I am so messed up right now." My speech was super slurred. I took a few steps and stopped.

"You okay?" He grabbed me with his other hand and pulled me closer to him.

"I'm good. I just had a little too much to drink."

"Yeah, I see." He laughed. "I think it's time for me to go, 'cause you are through. Do you mind if I take a shower before I go?"

"That's fine."

I surprised myself when I leaned down and kissed Brick on the lips. They looked so soft and I couldn't resist him any longer. When he kissed me back, it became more intense and soon, our tongues became intertwined with each other. My body was screaming and begging for his touch, so I straddled his lap with no hesitation. Brick's hands crept up my thighs and made their way to my butt. He palmed both cheeks and slid one hand inside my jeans. I could feel one of his fingers slide up and down my crack. My breathing was growing heavier by the second. With his free hand, he grabbed the back of my neck and kissed me harder.

Oh, my goodness, I wanted to fuck this man so bad.

On instinct, I rocked my body back and forth and dry rode his very stiff rod. We kissed a little while longer, but eventually, he broke our kiss.

"Why you stop?"

"Not like this. You had too much to drink and I don't want you feeling bad in the morning. I'm going to take a shower and leave." He lifted me from his lap. "Lead the way."

Brick followed me upstairs and into my bathroom. "You can shower in here. I'll get you a rag and a towel." I walked over to the chest and grabbed what he needed. "Here you go. My bedroom is right there." I pointed in the direction. "I'll be in there laying down until you ready."

"Okay."

I took a few steps towards the door, but I froze. "Give me your clothes so I can wash them."

Brick hesitated at first, but eventually he stripped out of every piece of clothing and a bitch was breathless, standing there looking all amazed and shit. This man was so damn fine, it didn't make no sense. I wanted to get naked right then and there and fuck him on sight.

"Stop drooling, ma, and get my clothes." He chuckled and handed them to me.

"Um. If you need me, just holla."

"A'ight."

My feet were stuck to the tile like I was standing in wet cement when he walked away. He had the sexiest back, with a large tattoo of the state of Florida, stacks of money and guns surrounding it and the words, *Brick Money Boyz* across the top. I knew his fuck game was strong and I wanted to find out badly. Finally finding the strength to move my feet, I left the bathroom hot and bothered and went to the laundry room to wash his clothes.

When I returned, the shower was still going, so I went into my room and stretched out across the bed. My mind couldn't erase that image from my head and neither could my body. Closing my eyes, I reached down inside my jeans and rubbed my clit, imagining it was his hand down there.

"Mm. Brick," I whispered to myself. My pussy was extremely wet and my clit was swollen. The vibrator wasn't going to do the job and I needed help. I moved my hand from my jeans, jumped to my feet and took off my clothes. This was my last chance to get what I wanted.

I walked into the bathroom and stood in front of the glass shower door for a few seconds, before I opened it. He was in the middle of lathering up his perfectly sculpted body, but he stopped the moment he saw me standing there in the nude. His eyes widened and I didn't know what to expect. All I knew was that I didn't want to be rejected the second time around.

"Damn." Brick rolled his tongue across his top lip, as he stroked his dick slowly with the washcloth.

"Can I join you?"

"Hell yeah," he replied, so I stepped into the shower, closed the door behind me and stood in front of him, awaiting his next move.

Right away, his lips touched mine and our tongues connected, picking up where we left off. Normally, I wouldn't get my hair wet, but tonight I was making an exception. Brick backed me up against the wall, pressing his body hard against mine. The only thing standing between us was his immensely large erection and I was anxious to feel it inside of me. Slowly easing my hand between my stomach and his, I took ahold of his anaconda to see how it felt in my hand, while rubbing my thumb across the sticky tip, smearing his oozing pre-cum. The head was fat as hell and I imagined wrapping my lips around his thick monster.

Brick scooped me into the air with his arms underneath my legs, keeping my back against the wall. Then, he used one of his hands to guide his throbbing dick against my sex lips. I wanted him and I wanted him bad. In between the kissing and heavy breathing, I had to force out my next sentence. "Tell me your real name."

"Brandon Riccardo," he answered with no hesitation.

Once he found my opening, he rubbed the head up and down my slit, making me wetter than I was earlier. With a quick thrust, he forced his way into my slippery tight tunnel, stretching me wide open like a born-again virgin.

"Ahhhhh." I held that note as he sunk deeper and deeper into Pandora's Box.

Brick held my legs and pumped in and out of me in slow motion. My back smoothly slid up and down the marble tile with ease. The warm water from the shower splashed all over our bodies and faces, while he stroked the hell out of my inner core. It was what I desired, more like needed.

"Ahh. Mm. Sss."

When he released my legs, I unconsciously wrapped them around his waist. Gripping both cheeks, he squeezed them roughly, forcing me down further onto his pipe. Our motions were on one accord and I matched him thrust for thrust.

"Ooh yeah. Fuck," I whined loudly. "Fuck me just like this."

That was the ammunition needed to increase his pace and the sexy moans coming from my voice box. My hands caressed the back of his neck, until he hit that spot that made me squeeze his neck hard, sending my nails into his flesh. The intensity of the strokes kept my mouth wide open, welcoming the water. I swallowed some and spit out the rest.

"This dick feel good to you, don't it?"

"Yes. Yes," I cried, stroking his ego. "It feels so good." I held onto his neck like I was riding a bull and didn't want to fall off.

"This the best dick I ever had in my life." I was telling the truth too. My breathing was so heavy and in my throat, I probably sounded like a drunk-ass dude, but I didn't care.

Our lips touched, he licked my lips and my hips twirled. "Hell yeah. Grind on that dick, baby."

Our chemistry was crazy and I peeped that before the liquor. His personality captivated me the second he threatened me. It was what he said that blew me away.

"Damn, you a pretty muthafucka. Believe me, ma, I don't wanna hurt you, but if I have to I will." He stroked my chin with his finger. *"Just don't do no stupid shit and I won't blow this pretty-ass face away."*

As crazy and psychotic it may sound, that shit turned me on. Our bodies moved to the same rhythm like synchronized swimmers as I continued to thrust my pelvis against his. Brick raised my body, pulled out of me and placed me on my feet. He placed his hand on my waist and turned me around so I could face the wall. I knew what time it was, so I placed both hands on the wall. My legs shook in anticipation when he tried to enter me from behind. Our heights were conflicting, so that made the task a little bit harder. After a few failed attempts, I guided him to the little bench in the corner of the shower and assumed the position.

Taken completely off guard, my heart sped up when he lifted my thighs into midair, resting them on his thighs. The penetration made my body scream, but I adjusted to him naturally. At first, he started with a slow grind until I was comfortable, then he switched it up on my ass and pounded the juice out the box. I felt every single inch of him in my stomach.

"Ahh. Ooh. Ooh. Shit," I screamed, then bit down on my lip in hopes of suppressing the pain, but that shit didn't work. "Ooooohhh."

"Unh. Unh. Don't whine now, this what you wanted." Gripping my waist tighter, he fucked me harder. "Take all this dick," he grunted. "This some good ass pwussy," he shouted.

Brick grunted and growled like the king of the jungle for a good amount of time. As soon as the noise stopped, he pulled out and smacked his dick against my ass where he released all of his cum. He let me down and we both took a deep breath, a few of them. When I turned around to face him, he was leaning against the wall smiling at me.

"You straight now?"

"I am now, thanks to you."

"Glad I could help with that."

Brick picked up his rag and bathed himself, while I grabbed my hand towel to lather it up. "Let me do that for you."

The man took my towel and washed my body thoroughly, including the area he manhandled. A chick was in heaven. After we were both all cleaned up, he followed me to the closet to get a bathrobe. He slipped it over his broad shoulders and tied it at the waist. I did the same.

"Thanks, beautiful."

"You're welcome." A chick couldn't stop blushing, 'cause his ass could definitely compliment me for the rest of the night and any day after that. "I'm going to put your clothes in the dryer. I'll be right back."

"A'ight."

"Make yourself comfortable."

Feeling like a new woman, I spun on my heels and rushed to the laundry room. Quickly tossing his clothes into the dryer, I made a mad dash back to the bedroom. When I crossed the threshold, my real-life sex doll was lying across the bed, doing something in his phone. Instead of interrupting him, I simply positioned myself beside all of that chocolate. The way he had me feeling after he put it down, I was ready to go a few more rounds, then wake up and make a big breakfast. We laid there in silence for what I guessed to be ten minutes. I thought he had fallen asleep.

"How much longer before my clothes are ready?" He stopped what he was doing and sat the phone beside him, giving me eye contact.

"They should be ready in ten to fifteen minutes." My body pillow was in arm's reach, so I pulled it close to me, resting my head on it and wrapped my legs around it.

"What's wrong?"

"Nothing," I answered quickly.

"You sure about that?"

"Yes," I assured him.

"You could've cuddled with me instead of that pillow. By now, you should know I don't bite, unless you ask me to."

Brick snatched my pillow from my grip and pulled me close to him. I found myself rubbing my hand across his firm chest. It felt good to be in the arms of a real man, giving me that safe and secure feeling. Lord knows I didn't want to let go and I surprised myself, when I did more than think it in my head.

"I want you to stay with me." My voice was just above a whisper, but loud enough for him to hear me. There was a pregnant pause in the room and suddenly, I regretted allowing those words to slip from my lips. Rejection wasn't my thing and I wasn't used to being told no. my inner petty wanted to say, *Nigga, I just gave you some mind-blowing shower sex and you wanna leave me?*

The room was still silent and guessing games wasn't my thing, so I decided to finish what I started, but as soon as I opened my mouth, he beat me to the punch with his laughter.

"Beautiful." He stroked my chin for the fifty-eleventh time. "I got you sprung already, huh? It's your turn to do the kidnapping."

"Hell yeah, it's my turn."

"When the last time a nigga hit this?" He slid his hand underneath my robe and grazed my lips. I quivered at his touch.

"Two years," I answered truthfully.

Brick grinned deviously when he heard my response and moved his hand to untie his robe. Licking his lips, he pulled the robe open slowly, exposing his semi-erection. "Ride my dick until I fall asleep and I'll stay."

Like the submissive female I was, I straddled his lap and made it my mission to leave him knocked out.

***

The next day, I was sprawled out in the bed and I was tired as hell. Every limb on my body was aching and sore and so was my sally cat. Last night's exercise had me worn the fuck out. Brick fucked me in every position humanly possible and made me cum so many times, I lost count. I would still be knocked out, if it wasn't for the sun and its blatant disrespect.

Slowly getting up, I looked around and checked out the empty spot his body occupied a few hours ago. It was cool to the touch, so I knew he had been gone for a while. I wiped the sleep from my eyes and pushed the covers back. The struggle was real to crawl out of bed, but I managed to push through with no problem. My first stop was to the bathroom, but he wasn't there, so I continued with my search throughout the house.

There was no trace of him ever being there. Not even his bloody shirt. It was like he just vanished into thin air. I went to the refrigerator and fixed myself a cold glass of orange juice and sat down at the table. That shit had me in heavy thought.

"Well, Zuri, you have proven yourself to be the silliest bitch on the planet." I sighed, moping over some dope-ass dick by a dude that held me at gunpoint. All I could do was shake my head and laugh. "Something is really wrong with this picture."

There was no doubt in my mind that after this, I needed my head checked. This had to be signs of *Crazy Bitch Syndrome*. Two years ago I decided to become celibate after ending my relationship with Kevin when things didn't work out. My ultimate decision was to remain inactive with my goodies until Daman walked through the gates. With my bad luck I couldn't find good dick between the legs of a good nigga that met my requirements. That was until last night when I found exactly what I liked and he shook me like LeBron James did his opponents.

My mind was racing so I jumped up, snatched my purse up and fumbled through it like crazy, before finally dumping the contents. As suspected, my car keys were gone.

"They're gone," I panicked with tears in my eyes. Then, I ran through the kitchen and into the garage. My worst nightmare had been confirmed, my car was gone. The police was gone have a field day when I told them he kidnapped me, fucked me for hours, spent the night and stole my car. Charlemagne the God would certainly give me "Donkey of the Day." Now all I needed was my phone, 'cause I needed my damn car back. Unless, his ass stole that too. So, I went on the hunt for it. Just as I was about to climb the stairs, there was a knock on the door.

Knock! Knock!

"Maybe that's the police bringing my shit back, or telling me it was involved in some type of criminal activity," I mumbled under my breath.

I snatched the door open with force. "What?" I screamed.

The gentleman looked at me and smiled. He had brown skin, long dreadlocks that went past his shoulders, and gold teeth. He was cute, but I didn't trust him. "Having a bad day already, huh?"

"Yes, I am. Now, what do you want?" I snapped.

"Well, I hope that changes for you. Life is too short."

My attitude was already fucked up and I wasn't in the mood for his sarcasm or niceness. "Listen, I'm not in a good mood. Have a nice day."

I pushed the door to close it. "Wait!" he shouted. "I believe these belong to you."

In his hand there was a very distinctive Marilyn Monroe keychain. "What are you doing with my keys?" I snatched them from his hands and took off, running towards my driveway. "Where is my car?"

My feet stopped moving when I made eye contact with my car. The window had been fixed. The sight alone made me laugh, 'cause I was acting like a plum fool a minute ago. "Ain't that a bitch?"

"I believe the correct reply is thank you," the guy behind me said, so I turned around to face him, all embarrassed and shit. "Brick sent me to fix your window."

"I'm so sorry for my rudeness, but I've had the craziest night."

"Ain't no pressure," he replied.

"Well, let me go and get my wallet. How much is it?"

"No charge, it's been handled. Have a better day." He smiled and took a few steps backwards.

"Well, at least let me give you a tip." My guilt wouldn't let me rest.

"Nah, Brick is my cousin and I would never take money from his woman. Enjoy your day, ma."

When I went back inside, I secured the locks on the door and leaned against it. "Who the hell is this man?"

My cheek bones were up high, blushing at the thought of him referring to me as his woman. If it was like that, then why did he leave and not give me his number? Then, I could call him, instead of him having me around here looking and feeling silly. I guess I would find out what he had in store for me, 'cause I was pretty sure this wouldn't be the last time I heard from Mr. Brandon Riccardo, aka Brick.

Chapter 4

Brick

After I slipped away from Zuri, I rolled up on my cousin Gucci that hustled in the city and fixed windows on the side. That was his way of proving a legitimate source of income. It was hard to prove expensive merchandise in the court of law without a job. After the way Zuri and I fucked all night, I had to send him over there while I went to the mall. It was only right I set her straight. He texted me when he was done and said he was on his way, so I headed back to the city.

Gucci sold drugs out of the Federal Apartments in the city and word on the street was that he was holding big. Niggas wasn't trying him, because he had a team of gorillas ready to go to war for him. All he had to do was say the word. He had his area on lock and I was in the process of shutting down shop with the other areas and making these busta ass niggas work for me. After I finished putting down threats, after being home for only two weeks, I was gone be the *Godfather of Lauderdale.* I was on my *Scarface* shit. All I needed was a goddess by my side and I think I found her.

When I hit the block, Gucci was standing outside, talking to some chick with green hair. I shook my head and laughed, "Only in the city."

The hood wasn't as bad as it looked before I left. They had torn down a few of the rundown apartments and replaced them with some nice townhouses. *Let me find out the city was trying to do a clean-up in the hood and put all the niggas out.* I hopped out my car and walked in his direction.

"You got my lady right?" I asked.

"Yeah, I got her mean ass right." Gucci laughed. "She cussed my ass out too."

"What you did to her?"

"Shidd, she was acting like a nigga stole her car or some shit."

"Yeah, that's a long story, but anyway, good looking out on the window tip."

"It's Gucci, baby."

"Nigga, how the fuck you get out? Last I checked, they was trying to bury your ass in that bitch." I looked in the direction the voice coming from and recognized that it was Melvin from the hood. We slapped hands and gave each other a hug.

"They let a real nigga go, but shit, I only had five years." I was cheesing harder than a bitch. It felt so good to be free.

"Damn, it's good to see you. How it feel to be a free man?" Melvin lit a cigarette.

"It feels damn good. I know one muthafuckin' thang, I ain't going back."

"So, you ain't hustlin' no more?" He blew smoke out his mouth.

"Oh, I'm chasing that check. I'm just not going back to prison. That shit dead, my nigga. I rather be carried by six than to be judged by twelve."

"Shit was that bad?"

"Nah, but that ain't no way to live. I hate being 'round ho' ass niggas all day. I need pussy and them fed ho's want too much. A bitch tried to finesse me, I had to tell that ho' to google me."

Melvin and Gucci were cracking up. "When you touched down?" Melvin asked.

"Two weeks ago."

"Damn, I thought you just got out." Melvin flicked his cigarette butt towards the road.

"Nah, I been laying low and strategizing."

"So, you ready to work?" Gucci nodded his head, awaiting my answer.

He had me fucked up fa sho. "Work?" I frowned. "Nigga, do I look like a goddamn worker? I'ma boss. Always have been, always will be. Fuck outta here with that worker shit, bruh."

Gucci frowned. "Calm down, nigga, damn." The chick with the green hair walked off and I was glad, because I got tired of that ugly-ass bitch, looking me dead in my mouth looking like the Grinch that stole Christmas.

I looked Gucci's ass up and down. He knew not to play with me. "Stop testing my gangster."

"Man, let's go to the liquor store." Gucci's car was parked closer than mine, so we took his car.

Gucci pulled out the parking lot. "The drug game has completely changed out here. Competition ain't what it used to be. Everybody too busy busting checks and committing fraud. They go up top and come back with bands, but not me. I'm straight on that tip. You got some young niggas out here balling off that shit. The ho's even doing it."

"That lick sounds sweet. I heard about it up the road."

"I'm straight with my operation. I supply weed, dope and pills. I was selling flakka too, but that shit come with a hefty sentence. The shit ain't that heavy in the streets the way it used to be."

"What the fuck is flakka?" That was some new shit to me and in prison we hear about everything first, before it hit the streets like a virus.

"The most powerful shit out here, I'm telling you, that shit make a muthafucka do the strangest shit. They out here killing, stealing, fucking with the cops and running around this bitch butt-ass naked."

"That sounds like some fucked-up shit to be on. Shit, heroin didn't have the fiends bugging like that."

"It's cheap, so it moves fast. I have to get this money while I can. I have dreams bigger than Lauderdale, so I have to work smart to make it out this shit alive."

I sat back and listened to Gucci explain the new rules to the game and his soldiers. Before I left the streets, I didn't follow trends, I was a trendsetter. We pulled up to the liquor store, got out and went inside.

Gucci and I were standing in line at the counter when a group of girls entered. One of them gave me an instant headache. My raggedy-ass baby mama, Deja.

"Well, look what the cat dragged in." I laughed.

"The best thang that ever happened to yo' ass." She stuck her tongue out. "Ahh."

"I guess that means it gets greater later." She stood behind me. "And why the fuck yo' drunk ass not with my baby?"

"It's the weekend and I need a break."

"A break from what? Yo' ass don't work."

"None of ya business. If you so worried, you go and get her from my mama."

It wasn't in my nature to hit a female, but Deja would make you go there. "Go get my fuckin' daughter from over there right now." I put my finger in her face. "If anything happen to her, I promise yo' ass gon' be pushin' fuckin' daisies on 19th Street. Now, play with me."

"Fuck you and get yo' hand out my face, dumb-ass nigga. You ain't been her daddy in five years. Yo' ass been replaced."

"Bruh, let's slide." Gucci grabbed me the arm to keep me from hittin' that ho' in the mouth. She knew what time it was, that's why she ducked.

"Fuck you, pussy ass ho'." I hawked up some spit and chunked it in her face. Her and her friends didn't say shit.

"I hate stupid ho's, bruh. She so fuckin' unfit." I walked off. "She got one month and I'm snatchin' my baby from her ass." Soon as we got in the car, I fixed me a cup.

Deja was a great mother before I left. I don't know what the fuck happened between then and now, besides the fact she's salty about me not coming home to her. My first night out, I smashed after the club, but that was it. I ain't touch her after that. Deja left me hanging during my bid and was fuckin' other niggas. She claimed she wasn't, but I knew better. I didn't even bother to tell her I was out, so when she saw me, she thought she'd seen a ghost.

I was standing amongst the crowd, checking out the scenery. Times had really changed. I had never seen so many ho's walking around with so much silicone in their asses. Those celebrities had really made these regular ho's lose their minds. Natural hair, eyebrows and curves weren't good enough and some of these chicks had really taken it to the extreme. They had invisible waists with overly inflated asses. Some were lopsided and didn't jiggle. I wouldn't smash none of these chicks. I was lying, but I wouldn't take them serious though. When I saw a familiar face, we locked eyes and she looked like she had seen a ghost. I called her name, so she would know it was me.

"Deja!" She paused, but she didn't answer me, so I walked up on her. "Don't look so afraid."

"Oh, I'm definitely not!"

"Same ol' Deja."

"I can't think of a better person to be."

"You still got that slick-ass mouth."

"Nothing's changed."

"Well, can a nigga get some love?" I reached out and gave her a hug. "Damn, it's been three long years since you left me standing alone in visitation."

She pulled back. "Don't do that."

"I'm not. This ain't the time or the place. I'll save that for another day."

"Thank you." She eyeballed me. "I will say that you are looking good."

I rubbed my chest. "You know how I do."

"Still conceited, I see."

"Ain't shit changed, but my address."

"Who you came here with?"

"Gucci."

"Oh, where he at?"

"I left him at the door talking to some bouncer bitch dude." Deja started laughing. "What? That bitch look like a dude."

"You crazy."

"Come on, let me get y'all some bottles."

"Some?" Deja replied. "Are you trying to get me drunk?"

I leaned over her shoulder. "Damn right, 'cause we fucking tonight. I got a suite at the Marriott for me and you." She blushed, so I knew it was going down.

After that night, the only dealings we had was the exchange of my six-year-old daughter and she hated that shit, but I didn't give a fuck. The bitch didn't care about me and now the feeling was mutual and a hunnid times worse.

We made it back to the block and posted up while sipping on some Henny. A few niggas from the hood slid up back-to-back, in wet candy-painted cars and big-ass rims, flossing all they jewelry. I couldn't lie tho', it felt good being back in the hood wit' some solid niggas, and not those bitch made ones in the chain gang.

After they cleared it an hour later, Gucci and I was choppin' it up.

"Aye, you ain't seen Playa? I been tryin' to run down on that fat, snitchin' bitch since my feet hit the freedom soil."

"Nah, he been ghost for a minute."

"I got somethin' hot for that nigga ass when I see him. His ass living on borrowed time right now." In the middle of my conversation, some nigga was yelling.

"Aye, Gucci, let me holla at you real quick."

Gucci walked over to him. I could tell it was a smoker by the way he was dressed. Nigga looked like he ain't seen soap or water in a decade. His clothes and shoes were too big and he was dirty, a young cat at that. He kept fidgeting, so I kept my eyes on him and that's when I could tell he had something in his hand, but I didn't know what it was. The smoker shifted his body and I saw Gucci take a step back and say, "You better put that shit up, before I put a hole in your head."

He was holding a shiny object and the reflection from the sun revealed a pocket knife. I sat my cup down and rushed over quickly, delivering two blows to his temple and he hit the ground. Gucci stomped the nigga soon as his head hit the concrete. There was blood and teeth flying. We gave him an ass whooping he wouldn't forget. Then, I spit on the nigga.

"Get yo' ass up and don't let me catch you on my block again."

I saw some dude walking up and I thought he wanted some too, but he was asking Gucci if he was good.

"You straight, fam?"

"Yeah, damn smoker had a knife."

"I heard the commotion and came outside. I thought I had to help you knock a nigga out."

"I'm good." Gucci introduced us. "Beans, this is my cousin, Brick. He just jumped out the feds."

"Damn, nigga, tell everybody I just got out," I joked, as I extended my hand to dap Beans up.

Beans laughed. He was a young dude wit' some nappy-ass dreads that needed a haircut last year. "It's cool, fam, we all been there, except for this clever ass nigga right here." He was talking about Gucci. "Y'all get up out of here in case he brings back the punk ass city cops. You know these smokers are the biggest muthafuckin' snitches."

"You right, I'll holla at you later." Gucci dapped him up real quick, then we walked to our cars.

"Damn, a nigga too fresh for this shit. Two weeks out and you got a nigga fighting."

"Nigga, I would've did the same shit for you."

"Yeah, I know. It's Gucci, baby." We laughed.

"What's up for tonight?"

"Shidd, wha'chu wanna do?"

"They having a party at Escape tonight, so I'm trying to see what up wit' that. Ion feel like driving too far. Last time, a nigga was so fucked up, I barely made it home." Gucci leaned against his car.

"Yeah, come grab me from the crib and we can slide and we ain't goin' to no damn Troy's either. I don' feel like busting no guns tonight. A nigga trying to chill and see what I can run up on."

"Nah, nigga, I ain't fuckin' wit' Troy's. A muthafucka always leave that bitch in a body bag."

"Yeah and don't leave out the ratchet ho's. I'm definitely not trying to run into none of them dusty-ass bitches."

"A'ight, cool. I'll hit you up when I'm on my way."

"Yeah."

We finally got into our cars and pulled off. I was ready to get out in the world and party tonight. A nigga was still fresh out and Gucci was still trying to make me catch up on all the pussy I missed out on while I was gone. Safety was rule number-one, 'cause a lot of these ho's was trifling, so I had to be careful who I gave this diamond dick to. I've been known to fuck up a bitch's world after I put this rod in they life. I done fucked up marriages and all, but last night I ran into something different and let my guard down. She was a different breed, so I didn't feel bad for raw dicking her fine ass down all night. As a matter of fact, I wanted to slide up on her ass right now, but I changed my mind and slid up on the girl that had my heart.

Boom! Boom! Boom!

As I stood at the door waiting, the heat from the sun was shining directly on my back. I wiped the sweat from my forehead and checked out my surroundings. Shortly after I could hear the locks clicking.

"Who is it?" she called out.

"Brick."

The door swung open and Ms. Loretta had a huge smile on her face. "Hey, son. It's so good to see you." Stepping forward, she gave me a hug and I hugged her back.

"Hey, ma, what's going on?"

"Nothing much just sitting around watching T.V. and watching my grandbabies." Ms. Loretta stepped to the side. "Come on in and I'll get Bre for you."

I walked over and sat down on the loveseat. She was watching The Best Man's wedding, which was funny because I actually liked that movie. Deja's mom and I had been cool since day one. She knew I was a good dude despite the salt that her daughter tried throwing on my name in an effort to get her to switch up on me.

Ms. Loretta owned a house in Lauderdale Manors and from the time we met, she had always been a working woman until she was diagnosed with Rheumatoid Arthritis. Shit had gotten so bad that she had to leave her job with the school board and undergo treatment. They only paid her for a period of time and that caused her to fall behind in her taxes.

I could remember back when she called me crying, stating they were going to take her house if she didn't come up with the money. Deja wouldn't help her pay it, so of course I did it. I couldn't stand to see her lose what she had worked so hard for.

Overnight her daughter had become the nastiest bitch walking and I wish I knew that shit ahead of time. The only thing good from that relationship was my daughter.

A few seconds later, I could hear movement and when I looked up Breanna was running full speed in my direction.

"Daddy. Daddy." She hopped on my lap and gave me a big wet kiss on my lips.

"Hey, Princess. Did you miss me?"

"Yes."

"I missed you, too."

"Did you come to pick me up?"

"Well actually I only came to see you before I go home."

Breanna poked out her lip and looked up at me with the saddest puppy dog eyes. "Daddy puhleaase! I wanna go with you," she whispered.

That little girl knew how to lay it on thick. My night was already planned with Gucci. I thought for a little bit before I answered her.

"Okay you can go with me. Go and get your bag." Brenna hopped down from my lap and ran back in the room.

Ms. Loretta was on the sofa sitting down smiling. "She got you, huh?"

"Yeah. She know I'm a sucker when it comes to her."

She leaned forward and her expression became a little more serious. "Brandon, I'm happy you're home and I need you to stay out. Bre needs you out here. That baby used to cry for you all the time. She would see your picture and cry. I didn't think she understood, but she did. And Deja ain't make it no better and she still ain't doing right. All she wants to do is party and carry on like she doesn't have kids to take care of."

My head snapped. "Kids?"

"Yeah she had another baby." She looked at me sideways. "She didn't tell you?"

"No."

"She has a one-year old son."

"I never saw him at her house."

"That's because she don't have him. The daddy has him full time. I don't know what's wrong with that girl."

"Me either. But my only concern is Breanna."

It was like she heard her name and emerged from the back, so I stood up. "You ready?"

"Yes."

"I'll catch you later, Ma."

"Okay take care. See you later, grandma baby. Come give me a hug and a kiss."

Breanna gave her a hug and a kiss and we were on our way."

***

At my place, Breanna and I sat on the floor stuffing our faces with pizza and fruit punch, while watching Princess and the Frog. Father and daughter time was important to me and that was the reason I canceled my plans with Gucci for the night. The streets ain't love nobody, but my daughter did and that was why I put her first at all times. If I died the next day, the streets would mourn me for a week, rock my face on a t-shirt and pour out some liquor. Once I hit the dirt they would carry on without a nigga and my daughter would never see them fake ass niggas again. On the other hand, my baby would mourn me for the rest of her life.

The news about Deja having another baby blew the fuck out of me, but at the same time it wasn't my business because I was nowhere in the picture.

When the movie was over it was a little past nine, so I gave her a bath and got her dressed for the bed. The apartment had two bedrooms. I made sure I had space for my princess. It had been so long since I saw her I wanted her with me as much as possible.

Flicking on the light, Breanna walked into her Disney Princess room and ran to her pink carriage shaped bed and dived onto it. The lady at Rooms to Go hooked me up. I had no idea how I wanted her room to look, so she helped me out in that department with the complete bedroom set. For the accessories, blankets and princess pictures I took Erin, my sister from another mister, with me to pick out the things she thought were suitable for her. And when they delivered the furniture she came over and help me set up everything.

"Okay Princess, what book do you want me to read?" I walked over to the bookshelf.

"Umm." Breanna placed her finger on her lip in deep thought. "Beauty and the Beast."

I grabbed the book and walked over to the bed and sat down on the stool. "Good choice." I smiled. "You're the beauty and I'm the Beast."

"You're funny, Daddy."

"I know." I opened up the book and got comfortable. "There was once a very rich merchant who had three daughters.Being a man of sense, he spared no cost for their education. His daughters grew to be very beautiful, especially the youngest, who was called Beauty, a special name that made her sisters very jealous of her."

Halfway into the story Breanna's eyes grew heavy, as she struggled to keep them open. Two more pages she was out for the count and snoring like a baby bear. I closed the book, sat it on the stool I was sitting on and tucked her in. Only God knew how much I loved this girl and what I would do to a muthafucka if they harmed her and that went for her stank ass mammy. Leaning down, I planted a kiss on her lips.

"I love you, baby. Sleep tight."

Before I left her room, I turned on her night light and turned off the lamp. Since I was in for the night, I fixed me a drink, rolled me a blunt and watched re-runs of Martin until my ass fell asleep.

Chapter 5

Gucci

I was sitting in my Impala, posted up in the Federals, chopping it up with Brick when Mehzani walked up. She was tall and slim, with some thick ass thighs. She was cute too with those beautiful brown eyes, full lips and gorgeous smile. There was only one problem though. She was hooked on that flakka shit at the age of eighteen. For the life of me I couldn't understand why, because she was a smart ass girl.

"Aye, nigga, you don't hear me talkin' to you?" Brick fussed.

My eyes were still on Mehzani. "Yeah, you said on Sunday, you wanna cop the werk from the connect."

"Who the fuck is that you keep looking at?"

"This chick named Mehzani. She a baddie."

"You mean, she was a baddie, 'cause she look like a pill popper if you ask me."

"I used to try and get at her, but she was always focused on school and shit, so I let her live. Shorty started hanging with the wrong crowd and everything went left. She was already partying with the drinking, but she started poppin' pills and getting loose with it."

"Damn, that's fucked up." Brick sighed.

"Yeah I know. I told my squad not to serve her, so I know that's why she here."

Mehzani was the only chick on that shit that made me feel some type of way. So, a few days ago, I had a meeting with my crew and told them not to sell her shit. I wanted to help her and I knew that would bring her to me. I rolled down my window so she could see me.

"Hey, Sunshine!" That was the name I gave her because that smile could light up the universe.

"What's up, Gucci?"

"I don't know. You tell me." I was so intrigued by her inner and outer beauty.

"I need to talk to you."

"Hop in the back and let's chat." She opened the door and plopped down in the back seat. I caught a whiff of her scent and I knew she had been out all night and day. She smelled like the sun and could definitely use a bath and a change of clothing.

"What's up?"

"I need to get high." I looked at her in the rearview mirror like she was crazy. "Come on, Gucci, please?"

"No, you need to quit doing that shit."

"Okay, what can I do for you then?"

Brick jumped right in. "Whoa, whoa, let me get out the car first. I'll holla at cha later, cuz."

"A'ight, man. I'll be through there around eleven to grab you."

"Cool."

Brick got out the car and closed the door. I then turned my attention back to her with a frown on my face. "Come on, don't do that, Sunshine. What I told you about that?"

"I only offered it to you. You know I don't get down like that, high or not." It sounded like she was trying to convince me, but I took her word for it until I heard otherwise.

"You know what the deal is and no, I'm not giving it to you and nobody else will either."

She folded her arms across her chest. "Yeah, I know. Your workers told me and that's why I came to see you.

Why are you doing this? I'm a paying customer and I never credit."

"Ion care about that. I don't want or need your money. I want to help you. Come get in the front seat."

She crawled across the seat and got comfortable, but I didn't say anything. It was only my slider car.

"Why do you care so much?" Mehzani pouted.

"In the beginning, I didn't care. Once I got to know you better, my conscience started to fuck with me."

"Oh, you have one of those." She giggled.

"Only when it comes to you." I grabbed her hand so that she'd know I was serious. "You're a smart girl, but you hang around the wrong people. You need someone to care about you and protect you. I don't need sex from you. It's a lot of ho's out here begging for the dick, but I'm not on that. All these ho's want is for a nigga to take care of them."

I knew she was affected by my words, because tears filled her eyes and slowly rolled down her cheeks.

"I want to stop, but I can't. It's the only thing that helps me escape the pain I feel inside every day. No one cares about me. They only pretend to care so they could use me."

Mehzani paused and wiped her eyes while sniffling. "I have no support from my family. I'm estranged from all of them, including my father. I haven't seen or heard from my sister and brother in years. It hurts that I no longer have them in my life."

"I care about you and your pain, and one day you will explain it all to me. We can take it one day at a time. I just want to take care of you. Would you let me do that?" She hesitated at first and just peered out the window for a little bit, before finally nodding her head.

"Is that a yes?" I asked.

"Yes."

We left the Federals and I took Mehzani to Target to get her some personal items, so she could shower. I promised her I would take her shopping in the morning and get her hair done. If I knew one thing about a female, clothes and a fresh hairdo would always make them feel better. Out of all the females I been through, she was the only one that had my heart and I never even smashed her. Behind my brown skin, dreadlocks and gold teeth lies a caring man that wanted to help a damsel in distress.

It was second nature for me to hop from chick to chick and they never lasted more than three months. There was something about Mehzani that made me want to rescue her from the grips of this cold, cold world. She deserved to be taken care of and treated like the queen she really was. Beneath that tough Teflon material was a delicate flower and she needed to be groomed.

I took her to my condo out west. No one knew where I lived and I planned on keeping it that way, 'cause I wasn't a sucker by a long shot. Brick didn't even know where I lived, but that wasn't going to happen period. I didn't trust that nigga for shit and I only kept him close, so I could pay attention to his every move. That's what you do when your enemies shared the same blood as you. There was only one person that knew where I lived and that was Melvin. I trusted that nigga with my life and he did the same with me. Loyalty ran very slim these days, so I kept everyone else at a distance.

While Mehzani was in the shower, I poured myself a cup of Patrón. It had been a long day and I needed it. I kicked back on my loveseat that sat off in the corner of my bedroom and put on some slow music. That was how I relaxed at the end of the night. Anthony Hamilton's "Her Heart" played softly through the speakers. In my building, the majority of my neighbors were asleep early. I lived by a bunch of old and nosey white people, but we got along just fine.

When I first moved in, I greeted the ones next door and learned the husband loved Cuban cigars. So, the next time I went over there, I took him a box of the finest cigars I could find, Cohiba Lanceros. That was a little investment to make sure they kept an eye out on my spot when I was away and it worked like a charm. I introduced him to Melvin and let him know that was the only person he would ever see at my place, and to call me if he saw anything or anyone that looked suspicious.

The lyrics sang to my soul and it made me emotional, thinking about my mother. He was her favorite artist. She wasn't dead, but she was in bad shape. Several months ago, she suffered from a real bad drug overdose and spent the last three months in rehab, learning to walk and talk. My family wanted to pull the plug on her, but I said hell no. I loved her too much to let go. It may sound selfish to some people, but you only get one mother and she had always been my backbone. I would never let her go without a fight. I had faith that she would recover one day. I didn't care if it took ten years. My ass was gone be right here waiting. I'd rather be able to see her face often, rather than going to the grave and talking to a headstone.

When I was younger, my mother was never on drugs, but all that changed when Brick came to live with us at our grandma's house, after his mother committed suicide when he was seventeen. Bruh was a loose cannon. He was selling drugs, stealing, and he wouldn't listen to nobody. My mom tried to keep him on the right path, but she couldn't since he blamed her and our grandma for his mother's death, claiming they didn't help her with her mental illness.

Brick got my mother hooked on drugs by introducing it to her during one of her depression stages after losing her sister. To this day, he wasn't aware that I knew, but I planned on confronting him about it and when I did, I was going to reveal my very own secret to him. The only reason my mother confessed was because she thought she was going to die and didn't go to the grave with that secret. That news hurt my heart because due to his evil ways, I lost my baby sister. On that dreadful night, my mom was so high and out her mind, the guy she smoked with raped my sister when she fell asleep. To keep her quiet, he put a pillow over her face, suffocating her in the process.

My mother and sister were the reason that Mehzani was here with me. I didn't want to see her end up like that, so if I could help one person, then I did my job. I had an airtight plan to get out of the game I wasn't supposed to be in, in the first place, but the money was fast and easy and I got too comfortable. Now, it was time for a change and I didn't want to be that man anymore.

Mehzani walked into the room and shifted my thoughts. Her scent is what grabbed my attention first. When I looked up, I froze. I was hypnotized by the way her shorts gripped her oily brown thighs just right. It's like they were talking to me, welcoming me to climb in between them and stroke that pussy nice and slow. My heart was telling me to look away and focus on taking things slow, but my mind said to go for it. There was a serious battle between the angel and devil on my shoulder.

"What's wrong?" she asked.

"We have to get you some bigger shorts." I laughed.

Chapter 6

Zuri

My weekend was officially starting and there was no way I was staying in the house tonight. Me and my best friend were going to the club and get our drink on. Brick literally fucked my world up in a matter of hours, and I needed a breath of fresh air. Just the thought of him being here gave me constant flashbacks about the way he fucked my mind and soul. My hands kept finding their way to play in my pussy every time I reminisced. *Damn, why he had to be so fine and gifted with that magic stick? Had a bitch hypnotized over here.* He had me ready to suck and eat that dick for breakfast, lunch and dinner.

I applied lotion to my medium-sized frame with Victoria's Secret Pure Seduction lotion and slid into an all-black fitted dress. I was exposing every curve on my body. This shit was thick. Not a big girl who doesn't know the difference between thick and fat, but a fine thick girl. I had no belly fat, toned thick thighs and a nice ass. It wasn't a big ghetto booty, but it was the right size for me.

I had nothing towards big girls, but some of them didn't know what to wear or what to cover. The ones with too much confidence would wear fitted dresses with a bunch of rolls, looking like a pillowcase stuffed with dirty laundry. A woman could be big and classy and still look sexy. Completely dressed, I stood in front of my full-body mirror and I was happy with who I was looking at. This dress fit me to the tee. I was about to turn heads tonight and decline all advances.

I put on a pair of stilettos and applied my make-up. My phone interrupted my thoughts and I thought it was Kyra, trying to rush me, but it was Daman. He didn't know about my plans, but he was sure as hell about to find out.

I used to go out all the time in the beginning of his bid, but now I didn't go anywhere, because he wanted me to stay home. But, I was going out tonight and have some fun for a change. He thought he was slick, calling me on video chat.

Daman was smiling, until he saw that I was wearing make-up. "And, where do you think you going?"

"I'm going to the club."

"You didn't ask me could you go anywhere."

I smirked. "I wasn't aware that I needed permission." The dick made me bold and I wasn't trying to hear none of that shit he was talking. My only concern was going out, getting drunk, coming back horny and making myself bust multiple orgasms. Although, I would prefer it if Brick would come back and make me climb the walls.

"Zuri, don't start this shit tonight. Take off that shit 'cause you ain't going nowhere!" he yelled.

"Why should I? I'm tired of sitting in here seven days a week, doing nothing. You call whenever you get ready and you expect me to just sit and look stupid, waiting aimlessly for your calls. You probably cheating anyway."

"You know damn well that's a lie. I don't have to cheat, and what the hell would I do with two complaining ass women? I can't handle your mouth at times. So, miss me with that cheating shit and besides, I'm in prison. What the fuck can I do in here, besides get money and take care of you?"

I knew he wasn't cheating, but I wasn't about to tell him that. I just wanted to start an argument, so he would hang up.

"Yeah, you take care of me financially, but what about mentally, physically and emotionally?" By this time, I was yelling because it was all true.

"We have a new warden, so what you want me to do? It ain't like it was during the first four years of my sentence. All I can give you is phone sex."

I looked at him like he was stupid. "And, you say that like it's enough. Figure it out like you do everything else."

"I can't tell. Not by the way you were calling out to God and anybody that was listening." Daman took a deep breath and closed his eyes.

"I'm sorry. I didn't mean for that to come out that way." Daman shot daggers through the phone. I could tell that he wasn't looking at me, but through me. I've been with him long enough to know that he would be giving me the silent treatment for the next few days.

"You said exactly what you mean, so don't apologize. I hope you find exactly what you looking for in the club." Daman ended the call without another word.

I felt like shit, because I didn't intend for it to escalate so far, but staying in the house still wasn't an option either. I had to go out. It would defeat the purpose of starting the argument in the first place. I grabbed my house keys and clutch purse, and headed downstairs. I needed to get wasted and fast. When I got in my car, I called Kyra to let her know I was on the way.

***

Escape Lounge was lit as fuck. There were so many faces I knew from back in the day, that I hadn't seen in a while. Tonight, they were having a party and a comedy show at the same time. Comedian Jett Wilson was in the building and the man was a whole fool in real life, straight hilarious. We were friends on Facebook and we grew up in the same neighborhood, Parkway. He was the main reason I came out in the first place. It was imperative that I supported the home team. When he left the stage, he greeted me with a hug.

"Thanks for coming out."

"It's all love. You know I have to come out and celebrate the home team. Just keep up the good work and don't forget about the little people when you blow up."

"I'll never do that." Jett smiled.

"Good, 'cause Broward can use some positivity to represent us."

"Fa'sho. I'm 'bouta head out. I'll catch you later."

"Okay." He kissed me on the cheek and went on his way.

After the show was over, they turned the music back up and proceeded with the party. Kyra and I got up from our seats so we could vibe to the music, as soon as they started jamming that new Cardi B, "Be Careful."

I wanna get married, like the Curry's, Steph and Ayesha...

The waitress walked up in the middle of me rapping, holding a drink in her hand. Not to be sadity, but I tooted my nose up at her like she was trying to slip me a date rape drug. "I didn't order a drink."

She smiled, while tilting her head towards the bar. "This is from the gentleman in the red shirt at the bar."

"Oh, my bad." I giggled nervously, slightly embarrassed and took the drink from her hand. "Tell him I said thanks, but I'm a happy lesbian."

The waitress bust out into laughter. "I will let him know."

70

"Thanks."

The dude at the bar was definitely not my cup of tea, soda or liquor, but I appreciated the free drink. Men that wore their pants tighter than me wasn't my thing, 'cause the day I woke up and saw him wearing my jeans, there would be hell to pay. Just throw the whole man away!

"Can you bring me a Long Island?" Kyra asked.

"Sure thing. Be right back." The waitress was overly excited like she loved her job, but I didn't doubt it. I was sure she raked in a lot of tips, 'cause she was fine. There wasn't a jealous bone in my body and I had no problem giving credit when it was due, unlike most women. She was the same height as me and had to weigh about a buck-sixty. The fishnet stockings she wore complimented her long legs and she had bone-straight, long hair down to her waist. She was what many referred to as slim thick.

I sipped my drink. "You should've got one of these, it's real good."

Kyra reached for my drink, so I moved my hand away from her. "Let me taste it."

"Uhh, issa no for me."

"Why?" Now she was acting clueless.

"You suck dick, that's why and I don't know where yo' mouth been."

She rolled her eyes and dropped her hands at her side. "Girl, bye! Ain't nobody suck no damn dick today."

"Well, you did yesterday and I know because you told me."

"Bruh, you so petty. You act like I didn't brush my teeth or some shit."

"Yeah, it's still a no for me. You have a drink coming, be patient, sus." I sipped some more of my drink. "Yeah, you should've definitely got you one of these too."

"I didn't know what it was and besides, you know I need my specialty to get me to my full ho' potential."

"Yeah, I know and that's why I refuse to drink behind you, 'cause yo' Ho-Fax report is off the meat rack."

"Don't judge me."

"Trust, I'm not. I'll leave that for the Lord on Judgment Day."

A lot of the time, I look at Kyra and I am speechless. One would think I was used to her behavior by now, but I wasn't, probably because I expected her to change over the years. This girl had no couth or shame in the things she would do or say, but it never changed the way I felt about her. Kyra was a cute girl with brown skin and she was a lot thicker than me. She had ass for days and weeks, which was why men were so drawn to her, along with her height. One could easily describe her as an amazon because of her five-foot ten frame. I just wished she didn't use her assets for free advertisement. Every piece of clothing she owned left nothing to the imagination.

It took a minute to realize she was going to be that way, until she decided to change. People thought since we were best friends, the saying, "birds of a feather flocked together" applied to us and that was a boldface lie. Kyra would fuck anything that had a pulse and wouldn't think twice about it. At times we had a rocky friendship, but who didn't? Kyra had some underlying issues from being molested, but she never spoke on them in detail. With the heavy flow of men running in and out their home I just figured it was one of her mom's pervert ass friends. Her mom had issues too and I remember when she sent Kyra away for a while, but then she returned months later. Whenever I asked her about it, she would shut me out and say her mom told her not to discuss their family business. Ultimately, I left it alone and stopped asking her about it. I figured she would tell me when she was ready.

When I went through my own personal issues with my dad, she was there for me during the whole ordeal without judgment. If it wasn't for her, I probably would've committed suicide. The media was eating the story alive and paparazzi tortured me on a daily basis, with the way they referred to my father as a monster and child molester that needed to be castrated. Our story was on every news station and advertised in every newspaper. The negative publicity drove me insane.

"Kyra, you should be tired of fucking on the first night and having one-night stands. You ain't gone be satisfied until you end up with the claps or some shit you can't cure."

"Girl, please. I ain't gone catch shit. You, on the other hand, need to start giving up that lil' bougie coochie. I know that bitch got cobwebs for days." Kyra was laughing and dancing in front of me, then she put her hand between my legs.

I swatted her hand away. "Stop, girl, wit'cho nasty gay ass."

"Stop being stingy with the puss and let a nigga beat that back in. You act like you sitting on a gold mine or some shit. I know for a fact that pwussy shooting out dust."

On the inside I hollered, 'cause I never told her about my encounter with Brick, the way he fucked my soul out my body and made me bust multiple, exhilarating nuts all over his musclebound snake.

"Fuck you, 'cause my shit came multiple times the other night. So, get 'cho life." I flipped my hair, while sticking my tongue out at her.

"Yassss, fish, that's what I'm talkin' 'bout all 2018, chasing bags, poppin' tags and busting nuts." Kyra paused, tilting her head to the side. "Hold up! Who you let run up in that?"

"None ya. Why you so nosey?"

"You always being secretive, wit'cho sneaky ass."

The waitress came back with Kyra's drink and handed it to her. "Thanks chi. I almost thought you forgot about me."

She laughed and walked off.

Kyra sipped her drink. "Damn this is strong. I'm 'bout to get litty as fuck. I'm going mingling. Keep those seats warm."

"I guess, chi."

For the next hour, I watched Kyra dance with a different dude every song. I guess she was trying to lock in her chosen piece of dick for the night, but I was ready to go home. There wasn't a single person in here that caught my attention and that was probably a result of Brick being on my mind all night long. His presence was taking up entirely too much space in my head. The crowd was steadily coming in and I knew my claustrophobia was going to kick in sooner or later. A huge crowd of people really got on my nerves and aggravated my soul. I needed to breathe. Kyra finally looked in my direction, so I signaled her over. She walked away from the guy she was dancing with. He stood there for all of three seconds and walked away.

"What's up?"

"I'm ready to go."

"Whyyy?" she whined and pouted like a damn child. "But, the crowd just getting here and I'm trying to see somebody."

"The dude you was dancing with left you."

"Girl, I don't care, that's why I walked away so fast. He got a small dick, so he wasn't going with me."

"Now, how you know that?" This girl was too funny and the sad part is that she was dead-ass serious.

"Girl, I been grinding all over him and I ain't felt a dick print yet. Make me think his ass a dyke in real life."

Kyra had me hollering at her comment. "Girl, you stupid. I can't with you."

"Nah, I can't with him. Out here flaunting that newborn baby dick."

My stomach was hurting so bad from laughing. "Bye, Kyra. I'm not playing with you tonight."

"Order another drink and I'll pay for it. I need to stay a little bit longer."

My arms were folded across my chest. "Thirty minutes and I'm leaving." This girl was legit getting on my fuckin' nerves, looking for some nigga she probably couldn't have. I knew one thing though, if she didn't have her next plan in motion in exactly thirty minutes, that ass was baked chicken because I was going home. My first mind told me to make her meet me here, so I could leave when I got ready.

"Ooh, bitch, he here," Kyra shouted and slapped me on the arm, scaring the heebie-jeebies out of me.

"Girl, get a grip. You so damn ratchet."

"Ask me do I care. Anyway, I'm going to get that, 'cause he too damn fine. Holla."

Kyra took off like she had a fire up under her ass. The only that was hot on her was her vagina. As the waitress was walking past me, I stopped her and ordered another drink. I might as well drink off her, while she try and talk a nigga up out his drawers. Now, I enjoyed sex as much as the next person, but I couldn't fathom sleeping with a bunch

75

of random niggas. I preferred finding one nigga I liked and sleeping with him, which was why I was so fixated on Brick's fine ass. We didn't have to be in a relationship, all I wanted was dick on a regular basis, with no strings attached. Just the thought of him had me squirming in my seat and fantasizing about riding his face. The last thing I needed was a wet cat with juices running down my leg in public. I wasn't wearing any panties, so the possibility of a rainfall was endless.

I spotted Kyra amongst the crowd and she looked like she was on the prowl, but I was unaware of who she was pursuing, nor did I care. My eyes continued to linger through the crowd of people that were coming in. When I stopped dead on the bouncer, I damn near had a heart attack. Butterflies rumbled around my liquor-filled stomach and my palms were consumed by sweat. My heart rate increased and the beat was loud like a drum major participating at the battle of the bands. This twenty-twenty vision had to be playing a deceptive game on me. There was no way that me and this man was in the same building at the same damn time. Rubbing my eyes, I tried to wipe away any sleep that might be affecting my vision, but when I looked again he was still there.

Lawd have mercy, Brandon Riccardo aka Brick, was in my presence and he looked better than he did a couple nights ago. My eyes were trained on him like he was in protective custody, as he bumped his way through the crowd until he posted up in the corner. True enough, he wasn't my man. But, after the things he did to me, I couldn't let that slide and I couldn't remove that from my memory bank. My nosey ass paid close attention to everyone he held a conversation with. We had unfinished business and I'll be damned if I let him get off that easily. Right about now, I was going through withdrawals like a meth head and he was the Methadone I needed to cure my cravings. All of them! My hot, moist and throbbing twat was silently begging and calling on him to put out this fire between my legs. When I realized he was finally alone, I grabbed my drink from the table and made my move. There was a bathroom close to where he was standing, so that worked out perfectly.

As soon as I was within several feet of him, some chick beat me getting there and she had this huge smile on her face. That shit pissed me off, because he acted like he knew her. My mind was telling me to turn around, but I ignored the suggestion. Just as I was getting ready to walk past them, he glanced in my direction and smirked. An uneasy feeling came over me and I wanted to run into the restroom stall and lock myself in there. It was awkward as hell to see the person that I slept with a few days ago, posted up with another female. If the sex was bad, I wouldn't care, but it was the best sex I ever had so I was in my feelings about that.

To keep it G though, I kept it pushing. There was no way I would let him see me sweat, although I was nervous as hell on the inside. My knees wanted to buckle so bad, but I had to stay strong. The ladies room was only a few feet away. From behind, I felt someone grab my arm, snatching me backwards and spilling my drink in the process.

"What the fuck?" I screamed, obviously pissed that I was about to bust my ass in those damn heels. When I turned to face the culprit, the hostility in my voice faded. "Why did you do that?"

"How you just gon' walk pass a nigga and don't speak after all that freaky shit we did the other night?"

Brick licked his lips and I wanted to fuck his ass on sight. He grabbed my arm and pulled me close to his body. The scent of his cologne filled my nostrils and I could've ate him alive. The way my nose was set up, I was certain he blessed his skin with Creed. *Damn, I loved a man that looked and smelled good.* His taste was expensive, because he looked like a Balmain mannequin standing in front of me.

"Well, I didn't want to get you in trouble and besides, you seemed occupied with someone else." The words flowed freely and before I could stop, it was too late. I knew I sounded all jealous and shit.

"For the record, Ms. Zuri, I am a single, grown ass man and I don't get in trouble."

"Sure you don't."

"You think if something was going on with me and that chick, I would be over here hugged up with you?"

Shrugging my shoulders, I grinned. "I don't know, you might have yo' ho's in check."

"I don't have ho's, baby."

"Good answer." All I wanted to hear is he's a free man. Soon enough, he would be mine.

Chapter 7

Zuri

Brick grabbed a handful of my ass and I was like putty in his hands from his touch alone. My pearl throbbed on contact, leaving my pussy sweating and sweltering. I closed my eyes, laid my head on his chest and bit down on my lip. The corner we were in was dark and empty, and I was ready to pull this dress up right here and let him murder this shit. I mean, *First 48* crime scene this shit. It sounded good, but I had to remain a lady.

"Did you miss me? 'Cause I missed you." His voice was deep and intoxicating.

"Maybe," I lied, playing hard to get. He didn't need to know I had been fanaticizing about him.

"Why you lyin' and shit?"

"You can't prove that," I challenged.

Brick didn't respond, but I felt his hand creep up my thigh. My eyes popped open and I immediately scanned the room to see if anyone was looking at us, but fortunately they weren't. The entire club was minding their own business. His fingertips were just as soft as I remembered, as he parted my lips and shoved his fingers inside my gushy center.

"Ahh," I gasped softly to myself. Both of my hands were at his waist, holding on to his belt.

His lips tickled my ear and I could feel his breath. "That's how I know you missed me." Brick pulled his fingers out slowly, then pushed them back in. He repeated that once more and played with my clit, before withdrawing them permanently. There was so much seduction in his eyes when I looked into them. It was like he had me under a spell. His fingers were coated with my juices. They glistened underneath the neon lights. Brick placed his fingers in his mouth and sucked them clean, like he had just finished eating some lemon pepper wings. If he sucked his fingers like that, I wondered what that mouth could do with my fat pussy in it.

"That's how I'ma suck that pussy."

A lump formed in my throat and I was speechless for several seconds. "So, who you came here with?"

Brick's eyes drifted away from me. Something or someone had his attention and I swore if it was a female, her ass was gone get dusted right now. I turned around and all I could do was laugh.

"He came here with me, mean-ass girl." Gucci laughed.

"I'm not mean and I apologized about snapping on you." They had some good genes. A few days ago, I didn't realize that Gucci was cute too. Maybe that was because he was in plain clothes.

"Stop harassing my lady, nigga." Brick eased up off the wall. "Wae the bottle at?"

"At the table, so let's slide."

He grabbed me by the hand. "Come on, baby, let's go get a drink since I made you drop yours." Without hesitation, I followed suit.

They had a table in the back by the pool tables. The first person I spotted was Kyra, hanging around a bunch of men that were shooting pool. I stopped in front of her, but Brick kept walking.

"Where you been? I thought you was ready to go, but I guess you found some entertainment." Kyra seemed like she had an attitude.

"Don't be a salty bitch, you been having fun all night and now it's my turn."

"Well, I'm ready to go."

"Well, that's too bad. I'm not."

"I guess, chi." She scrunched her face up. "How you know him anyway? It ain't like you be on anybody's scene."

"If you must know, I met him by my house a minute ago." Kyra was acting strange all of a sudden and that piqued my interest. My hand was now on my hip. "Sus, what's the problem? You heard something bad about him? You know him or smashed him already?"

"Not like that. I just heard his name ringing in the streets, that's all."

"Well damn, what you heard?"

"It wasn't nothing bad."

Stretching my eyes, I shook my head waiting for her to continue. "Okay, so what you heard?"

"I heard he just got out the feds and he 'bout his cash, that's all."

"That ain't nothing he didn't tell me. You would have all the tea on every nigga that gets out of prison."

"You know I do." She paused. "Oh, I thought you didn't like prison niggas?"

Before I could respond, I noticed Brick in my peripheral vision with a drink in his hand. "Here, baby."

"Thanks, baby." My smile was so wide, my cheeks were high in the air, damn near blocking my vision.

"Come over here with me." He pulled my arm and ushered me to the table in the cut.

"You just made me leave my friend." I took a sip of the drink he fixed.

"That's who you came here with?" he asked.

"Yeah."

"Gucci," he yelled over the music. To my surprise, he heard his name over the loud music and looked in our direction, raising his head like, *what's up?* "Keep her friend company." Gucci nodded his head and walked in Kyra's direction.

During the remainder of the night, we drank so many cups and danced our asses off that we were both sweaty as hell. Kyra was finally having fun once again, but a chick was tired, tipsy and ready to go for real this time. And, I'm sure Brick was tired of me teasing and grinding on his meat. Hell, I was tired of dry humping myself. The alcohol had kicked into full force and nasty sex was on my mind. All I wanted to do was suck his dick and swallow his cum. My ass was horny as hell.

I leaned in closely to him and licked his earlobe. "I'm drunk, horny and ready to go."

"Oh yeah." he chuckled.

"Hell, yeah. I'm ready for you to beat this pussy up," I whispered.

"Shidd, you ain't said nothin', let's ride. We gon' ride together, 'cause I didn't drive."

"Okay, but I have to take my friend home first."

"No, you don't, Gucci will do it." He stood up and tapped Gucci on the arm. "Aye, bruh, take her cousin. We 'bout to slide."

"A'ight."

We all left the club at the same time. My ass was taking baby steps when we made it outside to the parking lot. Brick kept laughing at me and slapping me on the ass.

"You drunk as hell. Give me yo' keys, 'cause you ain't driving me into a brick wall."

I pulled the keys from my clutch and handed them to him. "You wreck it, you bought it." It was evident I was drunk when I stumbled, almost busting my ass. By the grace of God, Brick caught me in his strong arms and carried me to the car. By the time he pulled off, my head hit the headrest and I closed my eyes.

***

Kyra

I couldn't believe Brick left the club with that bitch, Zuri. *How the fuck did she know that nigga anyway?* He had just got out the feds after doing five years. I heard all about the way he was getting money before he went in, and word on the street was he was back to reclaim what belonged to him. Her lame ass probably don't know him and just wanna get fucked, since her nasty-ass daddy went to prison. I saw his ass first and she knew that shit with her hating ass. That was fucked up! I always knew that ho' wasn't my friend.

My mind was dead set on fucking Brick, 'cause I knew he was gone be out tonight. I was keeping tabs on that nigga, so I already knew he ain't have no girl. Now, here I was sitting in the car with his cousin, Gucci, looking like Boo-Boo the fool. He was fine and all, but he wasn't who I wanted. My attitude was pissy, 'cause all my snacks had women, so they were in the house at this hour. One of them did want to come over, but I told him I was straight because I just knew that Brick was going to be in my bed tonight. He had a lot of nerve, pushing me off on his cousin.

We had finally pulled up to my duplex, but I pretended to be sleep. Gucci didn't know this, but he was fucking me tonight. He was looking too good and since I couldn't get his cousin, he would have to do. He walked around to my side and opened the door.

"Kyra, get up!" he yelled.

I blinked a few times to make it seem like I was out of it. "Where are we?" Knowing damn well I was home, but I had to make it look good.

"Your house," he said, sounding annoyed. "Now, get up."

I will say that he and Brick were just alike. They had fucked-up attitudes and were more impatient than a motherfucker. We made it inside and it was time to make my move. I took off my dress and threw it on the floor. I wasn't wearing any panties, so everything was out.

"Come on, let's go in the bedroom." I tried to grab his hand, but he moved it away.

"Go lay down, man, you drunk."

I rubbed my hands over my pussy. "You don't want any of this?"

He shook his head like I was really tripping. "No, I don't."

I walked up to him and got on my knees. I tried to unbuckle his pants, but he pushed my hands away.

"I'm out!"

"You must don't like pussy wit'cho gay ass, because no one turns me down."

"Oh, I love pussy." Gucci laughed. "I just don't want yours."

Gucci rushed out the door and didn't look back. I stumbled my drunk ass into my room and dove into the bed, head first. Looks like I wouldn't be getting any dick tonight.

***

Gucci

My ass was drunk as hell, but I had to get the fuck away from crazy-ass Kyra. A gang of niggas from the hood that was inside Escape kept saying how she was an easy smash, but turned into a stalker afterwards. I didn't want any parts of that.

When I made it to the crib, I was ready to hit the bed, since I hadn't been fucking nothing lately. I was too busy focusing on other shit. I took off everything I had on, except for my boxers and got up under the comforter. My eyes were closed, but I could feel my bed move. I opened my eyes slowly, only to find Mehzani standing over me.

"I was waiting on you to come in," she whispered.

"Are you okay?" I asked.

"Yeah."

She had this innocence about her that made me see past her addiction. I knew she wanted to change, because she didn't resist and she was still in place when I got back. Mehzani could've easily left while I was away and that was a risky move on my behalf, since I left her in my condo alone, although I had cameras. That let me know there was something deeper than me just wanting to help her. Shit, I just might love her. My main man, Mel, was on standby just in case she decided to leave or I saw something suspicious. I just needed to be sure I wasn't making any mistakes.

"So, what's going on with you, Sunshine?" That smile was everything to me whenever she blushed. Hell, it even made my dick jump, or maybe it was the alcohol.

"Can I sleep in here with you tonight? It's lonely over there," she replied, acting all innocent.

The drunk Gucci replied against my wishes. "Fa'sho, but that's at yo' own risk."

The way I was feeling, I was liable to slide in that pussy at any moment, I was already drunk and horny. Mehzani slid under the comforter and straddled me, taking me by surprise. It ain't like I was expecting her to be so damn bold with it.

"Sunshine, baby, please get up. I'm on this liquor and I won't be responsible for my actions."

She leaned down and kissed me. "I just want to thank you and show you how much I appreciate you."

"I believe you and trust me when I say this. I'm trying to spare you. We ain't ready for sex yet."

Mehzani stared at me with those bedroom eyes and scooted backwards until she was sitting on my legs, pulling my boxers down until my erection was free. My mind was saying no, but my body was definitely saying yes. My dick was standing straight up in the air.

"That's not what he's saying." Mehzani wrapped her soft lips around the tip of my head and slid down to the base, until she couldn't fit any more down her throat. The warmth from her mouth felt like I had just taken a dip into a heated pool. Her head was moving up and down, as I placed my hand on top of her head to slow her down. With her right hand, she stroked it up and down, while licking the shaft. Spitting on the tip, she kept on sucking, while stopping in between to slap her tongue with it.

Mehzani sucked my dick so good, my toes were curling. Her tiny hands gripped my balls gently, as she deep throated that meat until I could feel her tonsils. When I moaned out loud, I knew she had me. Shit, she knew it too. She had me moaning in the bed like a bitch, but I loved it. If she kept this up, ain't no telling what I might buy her.

When she slowed down, I reached over and opened the drawer on the night stand to grab a condom. I tore the wrapper open and tossed it on the floor, then motioned for her to stop so I could put the rubber on.

"What's that for?"

"No babies," I lied.

That wasn't the main reason, but she didn't need to know that. I didn't want to ruin the mood. The truth was, I didn't know if she had fucked anybody for drugs, so I'd rather be safe than sorry. After I strapped up, she slid down on that dick and that pussy was tight as hell. Maybe she wasn't ran through after all. I grabbed her waist and she rode it like a banshee. Her pussy muscles clenched tight around my pulsating stick.

"Ride this dick. Ride this dick good."

It was like my words were her motivation. Her body bounced up and down on it hard making her titties jiggle. With both hands, I grabbed them both and played with her nipples. Mehzani tossed her head back and closed her eyes, grinding me to death. Hell, I closed my eyes too and bit down on my lip. This girl was fuckin' awesome in the bed. The chicks I fucked couldn't take dick, so this was a first. She spun around on the wood without getting up. I licked my finger and stuck it in her ass.

"Oh, my gosh," she yelled. "It feels so good. Keep it in there. Please don't stop."

Watching her ass bounce up and down made me want to hit it just like that. I made her get into my favorite position, doggy style. The liquor had me in my zone and I was knee-deep in her pussy, with my finger in her ass.

"Ooooohhh, this dick so good. Fuck me, baby."

She took that dick like a savage, and right before I ejaculated I pulled out, snatched off the condom and gave that ass a semen shower.

Chapter 8

Brick

Dead and drunk weight was the devil, 'cause ain't no way in hell this woman was supposed to be this heavy. Her ass didn't feel like this when I was beating her down in the shower. Zuri was knocked out soon as I put her in the car. She was even snoring lightly. It was all good, she was still cute. Instead of going back to her place, I decided to take her back to mine. That should give her some security that I have nothing to hide, and my intentions with her were genuine.

Her girl, Kyra, was low-key pissed and eyeing a nigga with dirty looks in the parking lot, 'cause she was trying to get at me hard in the club, but I brushed her off and put Gucci on her ass. She saw my hand under Zuri's dress rubbing on her ass, so I blew her a kiss to fuck with her head.

Waking her up so she could walk on her own was a damn struggle. I don't know why I let her mix her liquor. I had her ass fucked up. That's what my ass gets, because I ended up having to carry her upstairs. I was thankful for the elevator. When I got to the front door, I had to throw her over my shoulder so I could get my keys out my pocket and unlock the door. The light from the kitchen was still on, so that made it easier to walk through, without tripping over the duffle bag I left on the floor.

When I got to the room and laid her in the middle of my California king bed, I was relieved. A nigga was too tipsy for all that extra shit, but I had to carry my baby since she was tapped out. One by one, I removed her heels and dropped them onto the floor. I knew for a fact them dogs was barking in them high-ass shoes. No one could make

89

me understand why women went through so much pain just to be cute. For good measure, I massaged both of her feet, only 'cause they were pretty. If she had those *Twelve Years a Slave* feet, her ass would've been up shit creek with no paddle and she would've woke up with socks on. As I caressed each foot she became more relaxed, so she had to be enjoying it. Zuri moved her leg closer to her body, giving me a clear shot of her pretty hairless pussy. I couldn't help but sing "Ms. Pretty Pussy" by Plies.

"Ms. Pretty Pussy, she can get it hot and gushy. Ms. Pretty Pussy, I like the way you twerk it for me."

My dick was getting hard just by looking at it. I already knew it was good, now I needed to know if it tasted as good as it looked. My mouth watered like this was my first meal in the real world. One leg was already open, so I pushed open the other one and ran my finger over her clit in a circular motion. While a nigga was locked up, I used to dream about devouring some cat when I touched down, but since I didn't trust Deja's funky ass, I waited. Regardless of the way I met Zuri and the short amount of time we've known each other, I trusted her. So, I didn't have a problem smashing her raw or eating the twat.

Ready to dive in, I got down to her level and inhaled her scent. That shit smelled like water, no smell at all. *Oh yeah, she edible!* Using my thumbs to spread her lips open, I slid my tongue across her opening. That thang was pink like cotton candy, sweet like it too. I flicked my tongue up and down like my shit was a paintbrush. Zuri squirmed in her sleep and a slight moan escaped those soft ass lips. Her eyes fluttered when I nibbled on her little man in a boat. "Mmm. Sss," she sounded like a snake.

That thang was juicy like a mango as I slurped and suctioned on it like I was trying to make it dry. Her eyes finally opened, catching a glance at me in action. My tongue was fat, so I made sure I hit every corner. I inserted two fingers inside, flexing them in the *come here* motion, in search of that G-spot.

"Ahh." She bit down on her lip. "Ooh. What you doing to me?"

Her question didn't warrant answering, so I kept at what I was doing, sucking and finger fucking her at the same time.

"Cum for me, beautiful." My mouth was full, but I could still make my demands.

"Ahh. I'm trying." Her moans were sexy as hell and music to my ears. She closed her eyes, but I wasn't having that shit. Not tonight. I stopped munching on her goodies and pulled her roughly to the edge of the bed.

"Try harder." I nudged her leg with my elbow. "Spread your legs wide and keep 'em open."

Zuri grabbed her ankles, then I shoved three fingers inside her warm pussy pool. After I found that spot, I curled my fingers and let them do the talking. They were saying, *bring that pussy here, girl.* Zuri was trying to hold in that noise, but I needed to hear it loud like some Beats by Dre. Aggressively and quickly, I moved my hand from side to side, hitting that erotic spot again.

"Oooooh, shit!" she screamed. "Baby, I can feel it coming. Keep going. Don't stop."

"That's what I'm lookin' fa."

My fingers stabbed her deep and hard, constantly hitting that spot for minutes on end, but I wasn't stopping until I got the results I was looking for. Zuri's screams were loud, yet filled with so much pleasure. I was getting off just by watching her buck in bed, like she was having a damn seizure.

"Cum for me, baby." My voice was deep, as I coached her right to an orgasm. Her juices leaked slowly, before shooting out and squirting like a fountain. Her eyes widened in amusement.

"Hell, yeah. Let it go." My fingers kept working until the squirting stopped. Her breathing was all off-key, like she needed an oxygen tank. I pulled my fingers out and rubbed her lips. She was hesitant, but all that was about to change.

"You scared to taste yourself?" I licked one of my fingers first, then placed them into her mouth. "I'm a freak, so you might as well get used to this. "That's your first time squirting?" She nodded her head yes.

My dick was on swole and so ready to dig in some guts, I couldn't get naked fast enough. I pulled her back to the edge of the bed, pushed her knees up to her shoulders and dropped that dick right in her.

"Grrr," I grunted when I felt her shit grip my piece tight like a vice grip. It was so tight and wet. "Ooh, shit."

"Oww," she moaned, placing her hands and feet on my chest trying to push me up out of it. I put my hands on her thighs to hold them down, applying pressure so I could put every inch in there. I wanted to see that stomach rise and fall when I went balls deep in it.

"Sss. Oww."

She kept moving and squirming, and wouldn't stop until I finally let go. Grabbing her legs, I held them in the air and grinded slowly against her center, hitting every corner.

"Shit." I loved to see her lips grip my shit like she be doing her Kegels every day. Zuri had to have a snapper, 'cause I swear it felt like that bitch was biting my meat in there.

Finally dropping her legs, I took a few deep strokes and that made her sit up and grab my neck. "Ooh." She cried, "You killin' me."

So I scooped her up and beat that pussy midair, instant replay of the shower scene. That only lasted for so long before it slipped out. I didn't know how flexible she was, but I was about to find out. I let her down, so she could stand up. Grabbing her leg, I raised it just enough to slide my dick back inside and raised that muthafucka to my shoulder. My grip was tight on her thigh while I pounded away. This time, I wasn't stopping until I busted a nut. From time to time, I smacked her ass, making it clap. By the time I finished punishing her, my neighbors were gonna know my name like Trey Songz. Zuri didn't know if she wanted to call me Brick or Brandon. To me, it didn't matter which one she chose. She had permission to call me by my government name. Zuri managed to stay in that position without fighting me for about ten minutes, before I let loose, glazing her walls with my fluids.

**

The following morning, I stirred in my sleep from having a good ass dream. I didn't want to get up, but I felt this warm and wet sensation below my waist. Last night was wild, but I wasn't that far gone to be pissing on my expensive ass sheets. When I found the strength to open up my eyes, Zuri was face down in my lap, giving me the wettest sloppy toppy. To see my piece going in and out her mouth was a beautiful sight. Her lips were wrapped around the python extra tight, like she was trying to tame him or pull the skin off.

Destiny Skai

"Damn, this how you wake yo' man up in the mornings?" Her eyes landed on mine for a brief second to nod her head before going back to bobbing and weaving. "Shit," I coughed, getting my words stuck in my throat. I guided her head to guide her pace.

Zuri slurped and licked on the tip, while jacking me off slowly until she took me back into her mouth, making it disappear inch by inch. The tip of my head hit the back of her throat and she did some shit with her muscles that massaged it tight. It made me nut the fuck up, especially when she squeezed my balls at the same time. My damn toes were Crip walking in my socks.

"Damn girl. Fuck." Her ass had me moaning like a bitch, no matter how hard I was trying to suppress it. My fingers were massaging the shit out her scalp.

Zuri's head moved rapidly up and down, suctioning the shaft like a vacuum. A tingling sensation arose from my nut sack, traveling all the way up. The sudden urge to thrust my pelvis hit me hard, so I grabbed her head and pushed her down further to meet me halfway.

"Ohh, shit," I gasped. "I'm 'bouta nut."

Every thrust was on a steady beat. My dick and her mouth was having crazy sex. All of my concentration was on busting, so I closed my eyes until I started shooting off in her mouth.

"It's coming. Shit. Ahh." That didn't stop Zuri from shining me up, but my shit was sensitive. I tried to move her head, but she had me on lock in her jaws. That was making me crazy.

"Baby, baby, baby please, stop," I begged. My knees never buckled while I was on my back. Oh yeah, she *wifey!* Big facts.

Zuri released the hold she had on me and I was finally able to breathe. "Whoo!" I exhaled.

She laughed and crawled beside me, laying in the crease of my arm. "You sound like a girl."

"You tryin' to kill a nigga."

"That was payback from last night when you almost killed me."

"Bruh, I knew that's what you was doing. You nasty for that."

"I'm nasty?" She raised that fat head of hers. "I don't think so. Do you remember what you did to me? I almost lost my voice messing with you."

"Almost doesn't count and that ain't fair, 'cause I was sleep."

"Well, favor ain't fair."

There was something about the woman in my bed that made me want her beyond sex. Her lips were calling my name, so I pulled her closer in order to taste them. My tongue found hers and kissed her sloppily. Shorty had that effect on me and that was real talk. Before it was all said and done, she was gone be mine.

"See how I kissed you in the mouth with no problem after you sucked my dick?"

Zuri frowned and poked her lips out. "Why so vulgar?"

"I'm sorry, baby. Let me start over." I was trying my best to keep from laughing, 'cause she was legit pouting over that comment. "Do you see how I kissed you in the mouth after you rocked my mic?"

"Now you being funny." She slapped my arm.

"Nah." I flipped on my side so we could see each other face-to-face. "Don't be offended. I was only joking and besides, I love to see those pretty lips wrapped around my, you know what."

"Yeah, I bet."

"I'm a bonafide freak. In due time, you will get used to it after I turn you into one."

"In due time, huh?"

Being slow wasn't my specialty, but I was sensing a little attitude. I just didn't know if she was serious or playing. "Why you gotta say it like that?"

"Honestly, I didn't think anything would come from this. After we did what we did, you just up and left like it was nothing to you. I mean, you didn't say bye, you didn't leave a number or come back later, so I felt like it was just a fuck and that I needed to get over it. Then, my gullible ass sees you again after I thought I wouldn't and fell back into the same trap again, getting drunk and fucked, knowing damn well the same thing gone happen again."

The words she spit at a nigga had me a little heated after catching me off guard, but I knew I needed to evaluate my response before I said it. Instead of snapping, I put myself in her shoes.

"Okay, I deserve that, but believe me when I say it ain't like that, so you ain't gotta come at a nigga sideways. The way we met was just so flat out crazy and unexpected. I'm still trying to wrap my head around it. Since that day, I had been contemplating on how to approach you, because I wanted my second approach to trump the first one. But we ended up running into each other last night, and here we are again and that wasn't a coincidence. I don't believe in that bullshit."

"All of that sounds good, but we both know why I'm here. We were both drunk and that led up to us fucking. But, the fact of the matter is, I opened my home up to you and my legs, and you didn't have the decency to say nothing to me and you probably still wouldn't have, if you didn't see me. That's just how I feel. I'm just somebody to fuck and that's why you brought me here."

Now, that shit blew a nigga, knocking me clean off my muthafuckin' rocker. So, I eased up from the bed, this girl was pissing me off and I had a bad temper that she knew nothing about. The shit Zuri witnessed when we met was only a sample. Empty threats being that I wasn't going to hurt her as long as she followed my instructions. Shit could get worse and I swear she didn't want to be a victim to these hands. I could damage her in more ways than one. I glared down at her with piercing eyes and bit down on my bottom lip.

"I'm sayin' tho', if you feel like a nigga only wanna fuck, why the fuck you still here? I ain't kidnap yo' ass this time, and you here so you'll know where I live and to show you I have nothing to hide from you. A nigga ain't hard up for no pussy. I can get any bitch in Lauderdale to fuck and suck this dick, so don't get that shit twisted. In case you didn't know, I'm that nigga, so do your homework before you come at me like I'm some elementary school fuck nigga."

Zuri didn't know who she was fuckin' with and she didn't know how heavy my name was in these streets. Her ass better check my goddamn resume, 'cause I don't fuck off, point blank period. I walked off on her ass and went to the bathroom. All the liquor I consumed the night before was ready to come out. I stood over the toilet and took a long piss like a race horse and washed my hands. When I went back into the room, she was getting dressed. If she wanted to leave, I wasn't gone stop her. Maybe it wasn't destiny after all. There was sadness in her eyes, but I didn't give a fuck. Her slick-mouth ass tried me hard.

After putting on her dress, she came to my side of the bed, brushing past me and looking for her shoes and car keys. Once they were in her hands, she hauled ass in the direction of the door. I strolled behind her since I was in no rush and had no intention on walking her downstairs. Shit was going good and she just went flip mode on me for no reason. That's 'cause she was used to fuckin' wit' these lame ass niggas, the complete opposite of me. Females like that didn't know how to act when a boss graced them with their presence.

Zuri unlocked my door and snatched it open, slamming it behind her.

Boom!

She ain't tell a nigga bye or nothing. *What kind of shit was that?* If I was in the mood for the drama, I would've chased her downstairs and showed her what time it was. It was cool. She got a pass on that one.

Chapter 9

Zuri

"So, this is what we do?"

Daman was hooting and hollering like a damn fool. It was clear he lost his mind. We had a fucked up relationship and that probably made me a fucked-up individual for sticking with it. But, it had been going on for so long, I just got used to the fact that I was in a relationship with my father. My aunt always said I needed my head checked because I had been brainwashed. It was crazy to many, but at the same time, no one understood what I went through. A girl's father is her first love and he was mine. Then, I lost my virginity to him and that made me love him even more. Daman and I were engaged in sexual intercourse for three years, but overall sexually active, for six and that made it hard to walk away.

"It's not that serious, damn. I told you Kyra was too drunk to drive me home."

"So, why didn't you call me so I wouldn't worry? That was so inconsiderate of you, but damn how I feel."

Now was the time to refresh his damn memory, 'cause clearly he forgot what he said prior to me going out that night. He really knew how to take shit overboard and that really irritated my ass. "You said that you wasn't waiting up for me and that was three days ago, so why we still arguing about that? You tripping for real and I ain't in the mood for this right now."

"Hold on," Daman said, before sitting the phone down, leaving me to stare at the uncomfortable metal bunkbed. He was really making my ass itch, calling me while I was at my place of business with the dumb shit. I was already aggravated by what happened between me and Brick and he was making it worse by bringing up old shit. The past was just that and I needed him to forget about it and move on.

It ain't like I would ever tell him I was too tired from having sex all damn night until the morning, with a guy I met a few days ago, who wouldn't let my sally cat rest. And every time I thought it was over he was sliding back in me.

Whenever we had problems, he pulled that same stunt. Honestly, I really had no intentions on staying out late, but seeing Brick stirred up my emotions and I couldn't shake his ass.

"So, you ignoring me?" Daman snapped. I had completely zoned out and I never saw him pick up the phone.

"Can you please stop yelling? I have a migraine."

"No, if it was me staying out overnight, you would swear I was out fuckin' off. I get static from you when I'm busy working in here."

"Oh, my God! You are killing me." I sighed loud and hard, just to aggravate his nerves.

"Listen to me, take it all in and digest this shit. No grown-ass woman with a man has no business spending the night with her friend. This ain't high school and if you was with Kyra, ain't no telling what y'all was doing."

"What does that supposed to mean?" I rolled my eyes into the phone.

"Kyra is very giving when it comes to sex, so quit acting like you don't know your friend is a ho', and she running a non-profit organization between her legs."

"That's her pussy, not mine and that doesn't mean I'm the same way. I don't know what your problem is with her, but miss me with that bullshit."

He was really starting to piss me off, because *"ho'"*

was nowhere near my category and he knew that. But, if it was, then that means he didn't raise me right. Yeah, I cheated a few nights ago, but that was the very first time in over two years.

"Well, you did say you didn't enjoy the sex the other night. Maybe you found someone to fuck you right. For all I know, you probably didn't go to the club at all. I hope you used a condom. I don't understand you. I take care of all the bills in the house and you have the audacity to walk in there the next morning like it's cool. That's total disrespect. Do you know how many women want a man that do what I do?"

Just when I was about to respond, he put his hand up and shook his head. "Don't answer that, I'll tell you. I have pussy thrown at me every single day by these bitches in uniform, but I pass on it. They know what my pockets look like and they want it, but that ain't happening. I ain't giving a bitch shit."

"That's what you say, but that can't be proven to me, so don't bring it up."

"I can't control the way you think and I can't make you believe me, so if that's how you feel then, oh well. Honestly, it seems like you trying to shift the blame on me because you guilty about your actions from the other night."

I placed both elbows on my desk and rubbed my temple with my thumbs. Slow deep breaths were what I needed to calm myself down and think about what I was about to say next. He wasn't going to be happy with this, but I didn't care. This was something that I had to do for my own well-being and Daman would have to deal with it. When I finally raised my head, he was just staring at me.

"Listen, I can't do this anymore. It's too much and you are really stressing me out."

"So, what are you saying?" Daman's bottom lip curled and his brow lowered. I could tell he wasn't expecting to hear this.

"I can't do this with you. I'm done."

"You can't tell me that."

"Well, I just did."

"You don't mean it," he objected. "You just pissed off right now and you need to cool off. I'm going to send you some money for lunch, dinner or whatever. Hell, maybe even for a spa treatment, so you can get'cho mind right."

It was obvious Daman wasn't listening to me. "Father, my mind is right and I have made my decision, so you don't have to send me anything. I'm good. This is too much for me."

"Oh, you being funny now." He scratched his head. "What nigga done been in yo' bed and between yo' legs to make you say that shit?"

"Would you stop assuming that it's a nigga who changed my mind? I am fully capable of making my own decisions. This is all me."

"Yeah, right. Yo' ass ain't saying all this for nothing."

"I'm saying it, because this has been on my mind for a while now. This is overwhelming and crazy and—"

"Let me stop you right there before we both something we gon' regret later. I'ma step back and give you some space, 'cause it's clear that something is goin' on with you. I don't know what or who, but you'll be honest about it one day. I'll still send the money. Have a good day."

Daman hung up the phone without me giving him a response. I didn't expect his reaction to be that calm, so that was a surprise to me. Nevertheless, I was happy that I didn't have to argue my way out, but it was still the hardest thing I've had to do in my life. Whoever put a curse on my love life could stop now, because I learned my lesson. No one could tell me that I wasn't going through this because of the love I shared with my father. I saw this as a punishment from God. Slowly but surely, it felt like I was losing all of my senses, as I banged my head against my desk.

"God, please help me. I'm so lost right now and I don't know what to do."

Tears filled my eyes and dripped onto my desk, making tiny splashes. All I wanted was to be happy and right about now, that idea seemed to be farfetched. At this point, I didn't know what I needed. Maybe church would be a good start, but those were filled with saints who swore up and down they never sinned in their life. I wasn't in the mood to be judged on any given Sunday.

It was only a quarter to eleven and I was already in a slump. Today was not going to be a good day at all, so it would probably be in my best interest to go home. My cellphone chimed, indicating I had some type of message. When I picked up my phone and unlocked the screen there was an unopened email, so I clicked it open. The message was from Google, stating I had just received five hundred dollars from Daman. I shook my head and sat the phone face down on my desk. That man didn't listen for shit, so that only meant one thing. Daman wasn't about to let go easily.

Gathering up my things, I decided to make it an early day and go home. I emailed my director and let her know I was sick. I never called in because I loved my job, so that wouldn't be an issue. There was no way I could do my job effectively with my mind corroded with a bunch of bullshit. After logging off my computer and locking up, I headed out my office. On my way through the hallway, I spotted Jason and tried to get away. That was the last person I wanted to see. When I got to the parking lot, I knew I was home free but as soon as I opened my door, I heard my name being called.

"Zuri," Jason shouted, while running in my direction. "Wait up." I tossed my things into the car and waited on him to approach me. "What's up? Where you going?"

"I'm going home." I sighed. "Today is not my day and I need to get away from here and try again tomorrow."

"Is everything okay?" He leaned against my car door.

"It will be. Just going through some personal shit, you know."

"I know the feeling, but you will be okay and I'm here if you anything."

"Thanks, Jason, I really appreciate that."

"No problem." Jason smiled and stood straight up. "You know I got your back. I'll call you later and check up on you."

"Okay," I replied.

"Hey, I was thinking that we could hang out this week-end. I hate seeing my friend down like this. We'll have fun."

"I would like that. It's time for me to get out the house anyway."

"Good. We'll talk later."

"Okay." He closed my door and waited until I pulled off.

Jason was one of the counselors at my job and a very cool person. We met about a year ago after he started and hit it off immediately. There was a mutual attraction between us in the beginning, but I pushed them to the side because I knew there could never be anything between us. For one, I couldn't betray Daman and two, I couldn't date inside the workplace. He probably would've been good for me since we were around the same age, but that was a thing of the past.

As I drove down Northeast 26th Street, I had a craving for something sweet. When I got to Federal Highway, I made a right and from the road, I could see the *Hot Now* light on for Krispy Kreme donuts. I was a sucker for sweets, so I ordered a dozen glazed donuts and went home to enjoy the rest of my day off.

When I made it home, I took a quick shower, slipped into some pajamas and crawled into my bed, sulking. The sad tune that played on Pandora was Jhené Aiko's, "The Worst." This song definitely had me in my feelings. My mind kept telling me I didn't need Brick, but my heart was singing and crying a different tune. *How could one feel so strong about a person they just met?* I didn't understand my reasoning for feeling this way about him. Sex was nothing, because I was capable of fucking without catching feelings. Whenever I came out of this slump, there were going to be mad changes. There were going to be stipulations on getting this vajajay. Nobody else was going to play me the way Brick's ol' stank ass did. My mind kept going back to him and that's probably 'cause I wanted to bust his ass in the face with a damn brick. After all of that thinking and eight donuts later, my eyes finally lost the battle to the Sandman and I fell asleep.

Destiny Skai

Chapter 10

Brick

The room was silent as I spoke to my newly formed team of killers and dealers. There were six of them total, including me. Gucci was there, but he had his own shit going on with his crew. He was only there because of his connection to the plug.

"As of today, Brick Money Boys is an alliance and we are in full effect and we take no prisoners. Keep y'all ears to the streets, so we can find and eliminate Playa, Legend and Marco. Those are the three that are standing in our way when it comes to the dope game. Them niggas in the way of me building this empire, so all of us can live comfortably."

I scanned the table to make sure everyone was paying attention and soaking everything up like a sponge. "Anybody that finds Playa, don't kill him. Call me instead. I have a personal issue with him and I want his blood on my hands. Y'all got that?"

"Got it, boss," they all replied in unison.

"Coop on the frontline, so if you can't reach me, hit him up and he'll tell you what to do."

Coop nodded his head in my direction.

"I have a shipment of dope coming in, so get in touch with your contacts so we can push this work. We selling whole keys for twenty and halves for eleven. Anything under that, y'all know how to add. Everybody in here got experience in this shit."

I looked at Skeet 'cause he was a rookie in the game, but Coop said the youngin' was loyal and a go-getter. It was time to test his knowledge. My phone was vibrating off the hook and when I looked down, it made me frown to see Dana's ass calling me. Last night at the club I shook her for Zuri, so I was sure that was the reason she kept blowing me up. I'll deal with her later. Right now, it was all about my business.

"Skeet, how much you selling an eight-ball for?"

Without hesitation, he replied, "That good shit goin' for two hundred and fifty."

"Quarter ounce?"

"Five hundred," he answered correctly.

"What about an ounce?" I tried to throw him off.

"Twelve hundred."

Needless to say, I was impressed and happy I didn't have to school this young boy. "Good job, young bull. I'll be paying special attention to you."

"I won't disappoint you and that's my word."

"We gon' see." I picked up my custom gold and black goblet that read, *BMB Brick,* and held it to the ceiling. "Pick up your goblets and join me in a toast." They held their custom-made goblets, filled with Ace of Spades, to the ceiling with me.

"Brick Money Boys is more than an alliance, we are a family and we will treat each other as such. We have no room for snakes, snitches, undercover beef, or jealousy. Those are the things that will make an empire crumble. We all about loyalty in here. Anybody doing otherwise will be eliminated, just like our enemies. Repeat after me; I am my brother's keeper."

"I am my brother's keeper," they all repeated.

"Down that shit." We all turned up our cups until they were empty. "Meeting adjourned."

I waited until everybody left, with the exception of my right-hand man, Coop, to address Gucci.

"Yo', what's up with the plug?" I turned my attention to him. "You act like you don' want a nigga to get on some shit."

"Nah, man, it ain't like that. I'm working on it, just chill out, bruh." He seemed a lil' fidgety.

"I mean, damn, another Sunday will be here in a few days and I ain't heard shit yet. Give it to a nigga straight, no chaser. Fuck all that beatin' around the bush and shit."

"Bruh, what the fuck I just said? I'm on it. I will introduce you. It ain't no thang. I'll be out the game soon anyway, so I ain't got no reason to do none of that shit."

"You getting' out the game, huh?" I rubbed my chin.

"Yeah. I got other plans."

"So, what you sayin', you handin' shit down to me so you can walk away?" Shit was about to get real. I could see the resistance in his face.

"You got yo' own shit moving. I was gon' pass it to my nigga on the frontline, Melvin," he coolly stated.

"Hmm. I see what it is."

"Don't trip. He been riding wit' a nigga from day one, so it's only right."

"Name your price and I'll buy that shit. That nigga ain't gon' be successful competing with me, so choose wisely." I looked at Coop. "Let's bounce, bruh." Coop got up from his seat and followed me. Gucci followed behind us and we went our separate ways.

***

After I dropped Coop off, I called Dana. She had been blowing up my phone and sending me crazy-ass text messages. I needed to check this ho', because she was out of line. Not to mention, Gucci had already called me and said she was trying to fuck him last night, when she saw me hugged up with Zuri. This ho' had the nerve to pick up with an attitude.

"Oh, you can talk now?"

"What the fuck you want? You been blowing my shit up for the past few days."

"How you gone leave the club with another bitch? That was so fucked up."

"Who the fuck you think you is, questioning me?"

"Brick, don't play with me. That dick got my name on it. I was the first one to get that when you came home."

"Nah, yo' ass was the second one."

She screamed in the phone. "You make me so sick. You fucked her too, didn't you? That's why you didn't answer your phone."

"Last time I checked I was a grown and single mutha-fuckin' man. And, I'm gon' act like one. I been down five years with no pussy and I'm 'bout to play catch up."

"So, that's a yes?"

"If you wanna know so bad, yes, I fucked her. I beat the brakes off the pussy too, but you already know that. You wanna hear that too?"

"You real nasty for that. I hope your dick fall off."

"You ain't my lady so fuck what 'chu talm 'bout. I can fuck any bitch without yo' permission."

She didn't respond when I said that and I knew she wouldn't. Dana was one of those chicks that wanted what she couldn't have, but I was here to let her know she could shake that shit out of her rabbit-ass mind.

"Don't get quiet now. You must want some dick?" I laughed. "A few fucks wasn't good enough for you?"

"Nah, I'm good."

"Nigga, quit lying. That ain't what those text messages was saying. You wanted me to come put that ass to sleep?"

"Why you play all day?" I could hear her take a deep breath in the phone. "You coming or not? I don't have time to keep playing with you."

The shit was funny as fuck, listening to this thot beg me to come over. At times, I knew I could be a ruthless, cold-hearted nigga, but I couldn't respect a ho' like that. If a woman wanted me to respect her, she needed to give me something to go on. Dana was willing to do anything at any price, so that meant I couldn't trust her.

"All you can do for me is suck my dick and that's it. I'll never stick my dick in you again."

"Oh, it's like that now?"

"Big factz."

"Fuck you, Brick. You ain't shit."

"That might be true, but you still want me to fuck you, fuck outta here, silly ass broad. Lose my number tho'."

Dana sucked her teeth. "Whatever!"

"Call Gucci. I'm sure he'll hit it."

"What the fuck I look like fuckin' Gucci?"

"He told me you tried to fuck him that night at the club, 'cause you was mad." She got quiet. "It's all good. I ain't mad at 'cha. Be easy."

I hung up on her dumb ass and blocked her number. Any other woman would've cursed my ass out. She was too stupid and simpleminded for me to even waste my time or nut on her. Dana had no morals or values and was too hell bent on what a nigga status was.

***

Destiny Skai

Later on that night, I contemplated on my next move. I was ready to set up shop and take it to the next level. Gucci, on the other hand, was satisfied with the way he had shit running, but not me. If he wanted to keep living like Mitch from *Paid in Full*, then that was on him. I was gone live like Tony Montana, fuck that. My goal was to expand and grow my clientele, which included taking over a few cities. There was only one issue standing in my way and that was Gucci. He was supposed to introduce me to the connect on Sunday, but he has yet to do so. I knew one muthafuckin' thang, if he didn't introduce me soon, I was gone rob his whole squad. Blood or no blood, he had me fucked up. That's one thing I hated was a lying-ass nigga. All he had to do was keep it a bill and kept it moving. I'm not saying that he would've got off easy. It would've made matters easier for him. Gucci was still that hardheaded jit from back in the day, but he felt superior because he was making moves. I didn't give a fuck about that cause I would still get on his ass. Oh yeah, we were going to have that conversation real soon. I had somebody on that for me, but I haven't heard anything back yet.

In the meantime, this lil' chick hit me up for some flakka, so I was headed to her. It was late at night and the breeze was cool, so I cracked my windows to enjoy the fresh air. South Florida was sunny and hot year round, so times like these needed to be taken advantage of. When I pulled into the complex, I parked in the cut and rolled up my windows. I was strapped and ready, just in case a nigga thought I was slipping. Lauderdale had turned into the robbing capital and that flakka shit was making these niggas bold as fuck. Every week, a nigga was getting killed in a robbery attempt.

112

I texted Mariah and told her I was outside. This nutty chick came outside skipping like she was on the playground. We met on the block and this chick was a real party animal, so we clicked instantly. We popped mollies together sometimes, but I wasn't on that flakka. That shit had these niggas and bitches walking around in zombie mode.

Mariah opened my car door and hopped in the front seat. "What's up, Brick?"

"Boolin'. What the fuck you skipping for?" I laughed.

"I'm happy and high, da fuck you mean?" She bounced up and down in the seat.

"Shawty, you wild." I sipped from my cup and sat it back down in the console.

"What's that?"

"Patrón."

"Damn, let me get a cup."

"It's in the back seat." She leaned over to the back seat and grabbed the bottle. I watched her fix herself a drink.

"Smoke wit'cha girl."

"Damn, my nigga, you want everything. Shidd, what I get in return?"

"I'm good for it, don't trip."

"I know."

We sat outside smoking and drinking for about an hour. We were higher than a muthafucka. I let my seat back to stretch my long legs, then dropped my head back on the headrest. The liquor and weed had my head feeling heavy. Mariah's hand crept along my thigh and I thought she was about to dig in my pockets, so I grabbed her hand tightly.

"What the fuck you doing?"

"Be still." Mariah unbuckled my pants, slipped her hand into my boxers and freed my Johnson. It was soft as hell.

"Aye, I done told you that you too young." I tried to stop her, but she kept going.

There was no sexual chemistry towards her on my behalf, but I could see she was diggin' a young fly nigga with money. I wasn't about to turn down no head from her, but it was a definite no on the pussy. Easing her mouth down into it, she sucked my dick slowly and sloppily. Mariah wasn't an amateur, but she wasn't a pro either and she sure as hell didn't give better sloppy toppy than Zuri. If anyone could hear the loud slurping noises she was making, they would swear she was a certified head doctor. But, shorty was only sucking the top half and that definitely didn't deserve a title. It seemed as if she needed help, so I pushed her head down and held it there until she gagged. My mission was to kill that mouth and hell no, I wasn't stopping because I told her out the gate her fast ass was too young for me. I told her to holla at me when she was grown. And, since she wanted to be grown tonight, I was gone treat her like she was an adult. I grabbed a handful of her hair and aggressively forced her head up and down. She was slurping and gagging.

"Don't choke, eat that dick. This what you wanted."

In the middle of my blowjob, a set of headlights blinded me, as it pulled into the complex. My eyes remained on the car until it parked a few spaces away from me. The driver emerged and my eyes widened like flying saucers when I saw this fat bitch get out. It was muthafuckin' Playa. I watched him as he walked like a sloth into an apartment on the first floor. My first mind wanted to go in blasting, but I didn't know what I was walking into. Oh yes, that ass was mine tonight, I grinned. My alarm on my phone went off in the nick of time.

"Mariah, stop. I gotta go."

She lifted her head up and I could see the pre-cum on her lips. "Why?"

As much as I wanted to bust a nut in her mouth, I wanted Playa more. "My girl just texted me, but we can finish this later," I lied.

After making Mariah go in the house, I sat and waited for this nigga to come outside. He was in there for at least an hour before he came back out. It was four in the morning, so there wasn't a soul in sight. I waited for him to open his car door before I ambushed his fat ass. I jumped in on the passenger side like a ninja, jamming my gun into his double chin.

"What the fuck?" He paused instantly when he saw my face. "Brick."

I smirked at his bitch ass. "Yeah pussy, it's me." I shoved the gun further into his skin and he started to stutter.

"C-come on, Brick, d-don't do this." He was begging me like the bitch he was. "I got a daughter, man."

"Fuck what you talkin' 'bout, you cost me five years of my fuckin' life. Yo' ass wasn't worried about me missing out on raising my fuckin' daughter, so fuck you. A nigga would've beat that shit if you didn't testify against me." As a torture tactic, I slid the gun from his chin to his temple. "Sending me away wasn't good enough though. You had to fuck my baby mama too?"

His eyes lit up like bright light bulbs in the dark. "Man, I swear on my daughter, I never had sex with Deja. You better talk to that nigga, Gucci. He was the one always at her house while you was gone. That shit was ringing heavy in the streets."

I let the shit he said roll off my back like water on a duck's ass. "Don't matter if you did or didn't. I could never trust a snitch, but before I kill you, just know that when yo' big ass hit the dirt, I'm rollin' up on her after school."

"Please don't kill my daughter, man. She ain't got nothin' to do with this," he begged.

"Nah, I ain't gon' kill her, but I'm gon' fuck her since she gon' be looking for a father figure. I'll help you with that. I promise."

With my finger on the trigger, I squeezed down on it and let off a single round in his head. Playa's body slumped forward on the steering wheel. Brain matter was splattered all over the window and front seat. A little bit was even on my shirt. The silencer prevented the gun from bringing attention my way. Word on the street was that he had just got back from up top and apparently was holding big. I checked the backseat and there was a duffle bag and a backpack. The shit was heavy when I picked it up, but everything must go. I looked over at his dead ass and checked his pockets.

"Yo' fat ass better have some real money in this bag or I'm coming back to fuck you up." Before I got out his car, I checked my surroundings and jumped in my car and peeled out. "Snitch down! The bitch is dead."

Chapter 11

Zuri

Tomorrow would make one week since the blowup with Brick went down and I had to admit, I was torn up over the way things went down. All I wanted was for him to see things from my point of view, and truly understand where I was coming from and how he made me feel. Out the blue, he snapped on me with no hesitation and without a valid reason. Maybe my delivery was all wrong, but I was speaking facts. He knew he was wrong and that's why he was easily offended.

Brick, Brandon, whatever the fuck his name was better be lucky I didn't have his phone number, because I would've called him and cursed his ass clean out for trying me like that. My feelings were hurt at first, but now it was full blown anger. The way he treated me was downright nasty and I didn't deserve that type of treatment. When I left his place my car ride was less than pleasant, being that I cried all the way home. Rejection wasn't a strong point for me and it had the tendency to break me down. Even as a child, I had that problem.

Life wasn't a walk in the park for me or my siblings. We didn't have a mother growing up, so we depended solely on our father to fill both roles and that wasn't easy, being a girl. Every Mother's Day, I would cry the entire day because I didn't understand what type of mother would just up and leave her kids without warning. Daman's voice played in my ears. *Why you crying over somebody that up and left you?* He was far from the sensitive type and that had a negative effect on me.

Daman was a very stern father and sometimes, he came off as mean because he gave tough love, but with that came validation. He said it was for my own good and it would keep me from depending on a man. I held on to his very words, up until the present time in my life and that was probably why I was fucked up now. *I'm the only man you will ever need in life.*

Over time, I constantly replayed his words in my head, and that ultimately caused me to be clingy and jealous when he would entertain women at our house. It took a while, but after a while, I was able to run every last one of them ho's away. That was no easy task, because he was a very attractive man and the women loved him. The thing they loved most was the fact that he was a single father. Daman stood at an even six feet and weighed close to two hundred pounds. His skin was a smooth brown and he was covered in tattoos, just like Brick. My daddy was fine and that was probably why I was so hooked on this handsome stranger to begin with. The day I crossed the line with him played over in my head.

When I was ten years old, I remember sitting in my father's lap while he watched the football game. Over time, we developed a closeness and that had become a normal routine. One day, I jumped in his lap, catching him by surprise and I felt his private part press against my leg. He moved me over, but I was already curious as to how it looked. That stemmed from me constantly watching my brother and his girlfriend in action.

Later on that night, I waited until he went to sleep to sneak into his room and into his bed. My brother wasn't home and my baby sister was sound asleep. At first, I was scared he would catch me, but I remembered he had been

118

drinking. He was wearing boxers, so that made it easy to reach for the thing that poked me earlier. Without an ounce of understanding, I put my mouth on it and did exactly what I saw my brother's girlfriend do. After doing that for a while, Daman eventually woke up when he made a loud grunting noise. When he saw that it was me in the bed, he jumped up, cursed me out and kicked me out his room.

My laughter filled the hallway as I reminisced on that day while going downstairs to refresh my glass. It was funny now because he was so mad at me, but back then it was painful to suffer from that type of rejection. My actions put him in an awkward situation and he didn't know how to deal with it. As I went through my teenage years, I truly felt Daman was the only man I wanted and needed. In my heart, I believed our actions were justified and there was nothing wrong with us being intimate. No one could tell me any different. Not even his meddling ass sister, who would tell anyone my business that would listen, the nerve of that cum-guzzling-ass ho'.

Now that I had been working for Kids in Distress, my thought process has shifted and my conscious was on high alert. Those children were one of the main reasons I broke up with Daman. It made me question my ability to help others, when I was in the same situation and happy about it. Hopefully, this new start will give me the normalcy I was in desperate need of, so I could live my best life. Since this new man stumbled into my life, he had taken up my head space and had me craving everything I've been missing. I was sure my attitude ruined any chance of us trying to build any type of relationship. So, with that being said, I was prepared to live my life to the fullest and with no regrets. Tonight, I was going out with Jason and chucking up the deuces to Brick once and for all. Whatever I thought was going to happen, was being pushed out of my head at that very moment. It was time to start fresh.

The ringing of my cell phone caught my attention. I answered it when I saw Kyra's name flashing across the screen. "Hello."

"What you doing, girl?" Kyra's voice was loud in my ear, so I put her big mouth ass on speaker phone.

"Girl, why you screaming in my ear and I ain't doing shit but sitting at the house, having a drink."

"You know damn well I talk loud, so stop the madness."

"Yeah, I forgot you ratchet." I laughed.

"Girl, bye. Anyway, what you doing tonight? I wanna go to the sports bar and get fucked up."

"Not tonight. I'm going out."

Kyra sucked her teeth. "Girl, who you going on a date with, the dude you went home with?"

She was irking my nerves already, 'cause she knew his damn name. That was straight shade. "Girl, quit acting like you don't know his name. And, if you must know, I'm not going with him. I'm going out with Jason and before you say anything, it's not a date."

"Yeah, yeah, if you say so. I guess that means y'all didn't hit it off. Let me guess, the dick was trash?"

"Kyra, I'm not going there with you right now."

"Why, 'cause you don't want me to know you let him fuck on the first night and the shit didn't work out?" Kyra giggled.

"You so fuckin' childish, dawg. Grow up today."

"Nope. I need to know if the dick was bap or nah?"

"Why, 'cause you wanna fuck him too if it was good?" Kyra made me pull her ho' card. I knew how she got down.

All the shady comments made me feel like she wanted him in the first place. When we first started drinking, I peeped how she kept looking at him, but I didn't think twice about it. I just felt like she was being Kyra.

"Ain't nobody trying to fuck him, girl. It was a simple question. I tell you my business all the time."

"The difference is I don't ask."

"That's because I'm not secretive and judgmental."

"I've never judged you," I snapped. "So, you need to quit lying all the damn time."

"You a goddamn lie. I peep all the shady shit you be saying. Just like at the club when you said, I'ma catch a venereal disease or some shit an antibiotic won't cure. You walk around like yo' shit don't stank and you don't have issues."

"Kyra!" I yelled, dragging her name and purposely cutting her off. "I don't know what the fuck yo' problem is, but I never said any of that shit. It seems like you just trying to start some shit and furthermore, I don't have issues."

"Girl, yes you do, but you wanna hide behind your job and house, like you the only one that can get that shit."

As I listened to her bashing me, all I could see was red and I wanted to fuck her up. She been felt that way about me. I was just too blinded by a long, fake friendship to see it.

"That's really sad. You the same jealous-ass Kyra. It ain't my fault you don't have your life in order and shit to show for the time you wasted in life. Maybe if you stop worrying about who paroling, or who getting out of jail and prison, you can get a job and move out the hood." I stood up so I could really give this ho' a piece of my mind. This was a long time coming.

"Jealous? Who jealous of you?" she repeated.

"The loose pussy ho' I'm arguing with. Who else on the phone?"

"Fuck you. You don't have shit I want or shit I can't have." Kyra was truly showing me her true colors and I was glad it finally came out. All these years she was low-key hating on me.

"Sure I don't, but that's why we arguing about it now. You been jealous since day one and my daddy used to tell me that you wasn't my friend, but I always gave you the benefit of the doubt. You want everything I got, including Brick. That's why you was so pressed about me leaving with him that night. Bitch, you wanted to go."

Kyra started laughing. "Yo' daddy. Girl, fuck yo' perverted-ass daddy. I expect him to say some shit like that, but have you ever stopped to think why he would say I wasn't a friend?"

Her words made me silent for a few, but that didn't stop her from talking.

"Yo' daddy been looking at little ass girls, so you ain't the first one and I'm sure you wasn't the last one either. His ass is where he deserves to be, in a fuckin' cage."

"My daddy ain't touch no other girls, so shut the fuck up. You don't know what the fuck you talking about, ol' dumb-ass ho'." She had me on one thousand with the shit she was saying.

"Girl, please come back to reality." Kyra was still laughing and being loud and obnoxious. "The man was a pervert, girl, and probably still is, so stop trying to defend him."

"Who did my daddy touch?"

"Me. Dumb-ass girl. Your daddy used to touch me all the time."

That shit hit me so hard, it caved in my chest and I didn't want to believe a word she was saying. "I don't believe you."

"Why, 'cause you think you was the only one he was fuckin'? Well, I'm sorry to bust your bubble, but he was fuckin' me for a year when we was in the eighth grade. He felt I needed to put out, since I was always at y'all house, instead of my own. You so damn smart, think back to that night he let us drink alcohol and you got sick. The next day, I wasn't in the room with you because I was in his bed all night, getting fucked in his favorite position, doggy style. And, if you don't believe that, he has a birthmark in the shape of a cherry on his dick."

"I guess that's why he said you ran a non-profit organization between your legs." I sighed. "Now it all makes sense."

The hand I held the phone with started to tremble and tears started to build up in my eyes. After all these years, this ho' had the nerve to admit she was fucking my daddy. I knew she wasn't lying, because I never told her about the birthmark. Our friendship was definitely over and I never wanted to see her ugly face again. This news broke my heart and hurt me to the core. Daman lied to me and I would never forgive him for sleeping with my ex-best friend. Both of them were history in my book. With my finger on the red icon, I ended the call and tossed the phone on the side of me.

Never in a million years did I think I would go through such betrayal. This whole time, Kyra played underneath me, when she hated me all along. Daman wasn't any better, knowing he lied to me on a daily basis. The day she referred to was present in my memory bank. I remember coming out the room to both of them with these guilty looks on their faces. They acted like they were some deer caught up in some headlights. At that point in time, I should've known something was up, but I was too naïve to peep game. I wanted to call Daman so bad, but I believed that was the universe's way of showing me I did the right thing by cutting him off. From this day forth, I never wanted to see or hear from either one of them again.

As for Kyra, it was on sight when I caught up with her ass, sus definitely tried it. All that slick rap was unforgiveable. Sometimes it was good to piss people off so you could see and hear the way they really feel about you.

Daman was right about her not being a friend, but he wasn't right either for fucking the person I considered a best friend to begin with. His old nasty ass.

Just thinking back to the night I saw Brick in the club, reminded me of the way she kept giving him the side eye, like she had a problem with him. Now I knew it was because she wanted to fuck him all along. All of her shady-ass comments and funny-acting behavior made it come full circle.

My mood was shot, but I needed to get out this house, before I lost the little bit of sense I had left. I needed to let loose, have fun and laugh. I knew Jason could make that happen, even when I didn't want to. He was exactly what I needed tonight. There was nothing or nobody that was going to stand in my way. Once Sunday came in two days, I was going to be in the house of the Lord with the saints and aint's. It was time to start over with a new peace of mind and live life like it's my last day. A text message came through and it was just the person I wanted to hear from.

Jason: Get ready. I'm on my way.
Zuri: I'll be ready ☺

Right after I hit send, I went into the bathroom, applied moisturizer to my face and took a quick shower. When I checked myself out in the mirror, it made me smile at the way my face was glowing. Back in the room, I applied some Diamond Glitter lotion by Bath & Body Works all over my brown skin. Its flawlessness was giving me life. I couldn't deal as it sparkled in the bright light from neck to toe.

A few weeks ago, I purchased this all-white crop top, with a tight-fitting skirt and tonight would be the perfect time to wear it. There was a lot to celebrate, so why not pull out the new fit. I loved the way it clung to my body and exposed my shape. Jason definitely better keep his eyes and hands to himself tonight. I most definitely came to slay and not play. I applied some lipstick to my full lips and oil to my plaits before pulling them into a side ponytail.

"Yasss girl, we ready."

I smiled and blew myself a kiss in the mirror. As soon as I was done, the sound of my doorbell chimed through the house. Of course, it was Jason, so I made my way downstairs and opened up the door. He was standing there with a huge grin on his face with his eyes bulging out the sockets.

"What you cheesing for, goofy?"

"Damn." He paused. "She's dressed for real this time?" Jason chuckled.

"Hush. I told you I was gone be ready this time."

"You know I didn't believe you, right?"

"I know. Come in so I can run upstairs and get my purse."

Jason came inside while I went back up to slip on my

sandals and grab my purse, along with my keys and cell-phone. I quickly sprayed on the body mist and went back down.

"I'm ready," I sang.

"Good, let's go turn the city out." Jason laughed, while opening up the door.

"I don't know about all of that, but I do wanna have fun." I set the alarm and we were on our way.

Chapter 12

Brick

Zuri was on my mind heavily and I couldn't allow another day to go by without apologizing for my explicit outburst. My bad temper got in the way of my understanding and I was too quick to jump down her throat, when she was only trying to tell me how she felt. It took me a minute to understand where she was coming from, now it all made sense. I just hoped it wasn't too late to get her back before she even gave me a chance to show her the real me. All of that was about to change tonight. If I could get her back, I made myself a promise to make her the first lady in my personal and business life. In my heart, I knew I could trust her and I had always been a good judge of character. Her loyalty to keeping our secret was confirmation that my life was safe in her hands in such a short amount of time. I was prepared to give Zuri everything she deserved and so much more.

As I cruised through her neighborhood bumping Yo Gotti's, "Pride To The Side," I glanced at the giant, stuffed all-black teddy bear, with the red bow around his neck and the beautiful bouquet of red roses I purchased about thirty minutes ago. This was the first step to make things right between us. A pleasant smile spread across my lips as I pictured her beautiful face when she saw me standing on her porch bearing gifts. As soon as I hit the corner traveling at a low rate of speed, my smile turned in an evil snarl and I was ready to pop off.

Zuri had her fine, hot-pussy ass on the porch, smiling and talking to some nigga like shit was sweet. My blood was boiling like hot lava and flowing heavily through my veins like kryptonite. She had me fucked up. My foot hit the accelerator hard, hitting damn near sixty mph. When I whipped into her driveway, my headlights blinded them and caused them both to jump. Clueless as to who was behind the wheel, they froze and waited for me to get out. I hopped out my whip and slammed the door hard behind me. Zuri's jaw hit the concrete when we made eye contact. Ignoring the cornball standing beside her, I stepped into her personal space and stood face to chest. She glanced up at me with a blank stare.

"What the fuck you doing out here, skinning and grinning in this nigga face?"

Zuri rolled her eyes so hard, I thought they were stuck. "Brandon, why are you here? I have nothing else to say to you. Goodbye." She tried to go around me, but I blocked her path to keep her from moving.

"Don't walk away from me when I'm talking to you."

"Just leave her alone. You see she don't want to talk to you."

I didn't bother to look in his direction. "Nigga, shut the fuck up and go get in yo' car, befo' I lay yo' ass out on this muthafuckin' concrete."

"Jason, please don't provoke him." She was giving his ass some sound advice, so he better take heed to what the fuck she was saying.

Ignoring her advice, he continued. I guess he thought he was running shit over here. "Zuri, let's go. We have twenty minutes to make our reservation."

My voice raised a few notches. "You ain't goin' nowhere, so stop fuckin' playing with me."

Zuri had the audacity to head in his direction, like she was gon' get in the car with him while I was standing there. This girl was really testing my gangsta right now. I took giant steps behind her and grabbed her arm, pulling her in my direction.

"Zuri, I promise if you get in that car, I'm fuckin' you up and you can bet that."

She stopped in her tracks and for the first time Zuri actually looked in my eyes. They were glassy like she was about to cry. "Why does it matter what I'm doing? We haven't talked since last week, so as far as I'm concerned, whatever we had is over. I gave you the benefit of the doubt and you ruined it."

Damn, her words sucker-punched a nigga in the gut, but I wasn't about to give up that easy and especially not to this cornball-ass nigga. I had no choice, but to adjust my tone.

"I was out of line that day and I'm sorry. Let's go in the house and talk about this in private."

"I'll call you tomorrow."

Zuri tried moving her hand, but I tightened my grip. "No, you ain't, 'cause you not leavin' here. What part of that don't you understand?"

If she thought she was cruising off into the night with Steve Urkel, she had another muthafuckin' thang coming. I didn't give a fuck how mad she was.

"Why does everything have to be on your terms?" Her voice was low and I could see her looking away in the direction of her friend. It was only right that I matched her tone, until she provoked me back into beast mode.

"Zuri, baby, I'm a man and that's how it's been since day-one. Tell ya lil' friend goodnight and let's go inside and talk about this like adults." I took her hand in mine and pulled her towards me.

Square buddy tried to pry my hand away from Zuri. My reflexes caused me to release her and aim my frustration on him. I cocked my arm back and punched buddy dead in his shit. His body flew backwards, crashing into his car.

Zuri screamed and rushed to his side. "What is wrong with you?"

"You defending this nigga?" I barked, stepping closer to them.

"He's only my friend and he didn't do anything to you." Zuri stood in between us. I guess she thought I was about to hit him again. That nigga was dazed, so she helped him on his feet, then escorted him to the driver's side of his car.

"He in my fuckin' business, so he did do something and you got three seconds to get over before I—"

Zuri held up her hand to cut me off. "I'm sorry, Jason. I'll call you tomorrow."

"No, the fuck you won't. I'll break that goddamn phone, now try me. Urk, yo' punk ass betta stay away from my woman and I mean that shit. I'm not repeating myself, so kick rocks wit' no socks, nigga."

Zuri stormed her mad ass towards the front door, but I didn't give a fuck. She could huff and puff and blow this goddamn house down, for all I care. I meant every word I said and she could take that shit to the bank.

"Girl, slow yo' ass down, fuck wrong wit' you?" She turned away from the door and faced me.

"You are what's wrong with me," she screamed. "It never fails, every time I push you out my head, you show up and do the unthinkable. So, thank you, Brandon for ruining my night."

Zuri pushed the door open hard, so we could take our argument on the inside. The last thing I needed was her nosey ass neighbor calling the police or coming over, interrupting what I had going on. Instead of waiting on me, she made a beeline up the stairs and I followed. Her last comment she made was funny as fuck tho', so I had to respond to that.

"What I ruined? Yo' date with Steve Urkel?" I laughed. "You must be crazy."

Zuri stopped at the threshold of her bedroom and faced me with her arms folded. The cold stare she gave me would've laid me clean out if looks could kill. "Call him whatever you want, but he made time for me by choice and not by coincidence."

Man, a nigga would've thought I was The Flash, the way I ran up on her ass and grabbed her by the jaw, glaring down in her face.

"Why the fuck you keep trying me, man? You know a nigga fucked up 'bout you."

She slapped me with much force across the face and the sound echoed throughout the room. "Get your fuckin' hands off me."

That shit caught me off guard. I wasn't expecting her to pop off on me, so I stood there and mugged her hard, unsure of my next move. Zuri didn't flinch, not one bit. She just stood there mugging me in return, looking at me like I was crazy. This girl had me about to lose my muthafuckin' mind and we wasn't even in a relationship.

Zuri's mouth game had me ready to murk sumthin' on sight and fuck her up too, with all that slick rap. Her ass talked mad shit, but I could never pull myself to hurt her. She had me feeling soft as hell. I leaned down and kissed her on the lips, but she didn't reciprocate. Yep, she was big mad.

"I know you mad at me, but all I want is the chance to make it up to you."

She pulled away and took a step backwards. "Why won't you just leave me alone and find you a ho' that will fuck and suck you, whenever you feel like being bothered, 'cause you don't need me."

I took a step towards her and placed my hand behind her head, then stroked the back of her neck with my thumb. "Ma, listen to me and I want you to let this sink in. I don't want no ho's, I want a woman and that's why I'm here, 'cause I want you."

"Tuh." She rolled her eyes. "You have a funny way of showing it."

"Listen, I'm sorry for blowing up on you. I overreacted and I'm man enough to admit I was wrong."

I reached down and took both of her hands into mine, one by one. Her body was still tense, so I brought her hands to my mouth and kissed them in hopes that she would relax. When she didn't resist me, I kissed her once more in the mouth. Unable to resist my hardcore demeanor she engaged in a lip lock with me and I could feel her tongue moving around in my mouth.

My hands caressed her pillow soft derriere and I rocked up instantly. It had been a whole week since I was grinding hard between her thighs and my boy was anxious to take another dive. I backed her up to the bed and snatched her up out that tight-ass skirt she was wearing. As bad as I wanted to address it, I decided to keep quiet so I didn't ruin the mood.

Zuri eased onto the bed and I put her on all-fours. She arched her back and tooted that ass up in the air. Her fat pussy was sitting up, motioning for me to come inside, as it dripped in juices. I couldn't resist putting my face all up in it. My tongue rolled slowly up her slit and back down again, before slithering inside her sweet nookie.

"Mm." She pushed her ass closer to my face and moved back and forth on it. Booty cheeks were shaking all in my face.

It was time to mount up and ride that ass, so I stood up behind her and entered that juicy spot. With a tight grip on her ass cheeks, I dug deep in that pussy. I wanted my dick to feel her heart beating.

"Ahh. Mm," she moaned and threw it back.

This time, I was determined to fuck her soul and embed in her mind how good I made her pussy feel. No man would ever make her feel like this and I was confident about that. My back was strong and my dick game was grade-A. In Pussy-ology, I passed with straight A's.

The sound of skin slapping turned me on, as it echoed and bounced off every wall. I went ham in that ass and she was hollering.

"Fuuuck!" she screamed, gripping the sheets and breathing all hard and shit. "Slow down."

"Unh-unh. This yo' punishment for trying me."

"My stomach hurt," she whined.

"Mine was hurting too when I saw you wit' that nigga." I switched angles, digging in it sideways.

"Oww. Brick." I loved the way she screamed my name.

"You gon' stay away from that nigga?"

"Yes. Yes."

"You promise?"

"Ooh. Yes."

I smacked her ass aggressively and it jiggled. "Say you promise."

"I promise, Zaddy. I promise," she gasped. "On Gawd, I promise."

"You belong to me now and don't you forget it."

"Yes, Zaddy."

Zuri sounded like her lungs needed some oxygen, so I slowed down a little bit and licked up and down her spine, while wrapping her hair around my hand. She was aroused and I felt her warm juices gushing all over the base of my dick. Zuri threw it back harder, so I stopped all movement and let her do the work for a minute or so.

"Damn, I thought I would never feel you again." Zuri had me moaning. "This dick good to you?"

"Yes," she moaned.

Once again, I was ready to stand up in that ass again. I flipped Zuri on her stomach, put both her legs on my shoulders, pinned her down to the bed and beat that pussy ferociously. She couldn't squirm at all, as I pushed all my weight down on her. Her nails were deep in my back, while she bit on my neck. That didn't stop my show. I kept going until I felt that pressure build up. It was too good to pull out, so I released all my baby gangsters in her uterus. I wouldn't be surprised if she got pregnant from it. Not that I wanted that to happen, but I knew the possibility was endless.

Afterwards, I laid on my back, staring at the ceiling with Zuri in my arms. It felt so right being with her and I knew I made the right decision. My heart told me she was the one, so I decided to go with that. Her innocence and loyalty captured my heart. Pulling her closer to me I kissed her forehead.

"There's no going back in time, but I promise that things will be different going forward and you won't regret it."

"Okay."

"You belong to me now. You know that, right?"

She nodded her head up and down. "I know."

It was official. I got my girl and I was gone make sure I took care of her mentally, physically and emotionally. We fell asleep to the sound of our heartbeats.

Destiny Skai

Chapter 13

Kyra

I was laying on my side, watching Jeff as he got dressed. He was one of my snacks that I had been messing around with for about six months, although he had a girl-friend, just like the rest of my snacks I was involved with. For one, I didn't care that they had someone and that was the reason I had so many of them. When one couldn't be there, the other one could. There were times where it got lonely and I would let my feelings get involved, causing me to act like a crazy, stalker chick. I wanted what I wanted, when I wanted it, so I was known to get out of character at times. And, I was well within my rights to do so, because we were doing couple activities.

A lot of my ways come from me not having a father in my life, and that always left me looking for love from some man, which ultimately led me to being hurt. So, to avoid being hurt by one man, I juggled many men because they all had that one good trait in all of them that allowed me to create the one man I will never find in one human being. Closing my eyes, I reminisced on the day that my life changed for the worst.

It all started back to my eighth grade year. I was filling out more than girls my age and so was Zuri. Older boys and grown-ass men would always try to talk to us, but we were only kids ourselves. They would hiss at us whenever we went anywhere and try to get our numbers, but we were only into boys our age.

One night, I stayed over at Zuri's house and I did that a lot because I hated to be home with my mom and her loud-ass friends. All she did was drink and have card parties. I was missing out on a lot of sleep, so I went where I could get some rest. In the middle of the night, I went into the bathroom and when I came out, her dad was standing by the door.

"Are you okay?" Daman asked.

"Yes." I knew he had been drinking because I could smell the stale alcohol on his breath. There was some white residue on his nose, so that meant he was high too.

"Come on. I want to talk to you about staying over so much and why you never want to stay home."

"Okay."

I followed him into the den and sat down.

"You know you stay over here a lot and I don't mind, but you have to kick out something."

I was confused, because I didn't know what he was talking about. "What do you mean?"

Daman rubbed his hand underneath my nightgown and caressed my thighs. "It costs to feed an extra mouth in this house and I figure you can pay me with this."

He was rubbing his finger between my vagina lips. I wanted to run back into Zuri's room, but I didn't. I just sat there and let him molest me.

Daman pushed me gently onto the couch and climbed on top of me. His breathing was heavy, as he made a few attempts to stick his extra-large dick into my small vagina. I wasn't a virgin, but the boys my age were hardly that size, so I wasn't used to it. When he finally got it in, it felt like he was dry humping me, because I wasn't wet. It hurt as he went in and out of my extremely tight walls. I guess he wasn't enjoying the dry feeling, because he went down and licked on my immature clit. I never experienced head before and it sent a weird chill down my spine. When he put

138

his erection back in, it was slippery. In my mind I didn't enjoy it, but my actions said different, because I was moaning. He put his hand over my mouth so no one would hear us.

After he was done, I got up and went into the bathroom to clean myself off and then I went back to bed. I never told Zuri about what her dad did to me and it continued for a whole year, before he stopped after getting me pregnant. That made my situation at home that much worse, but of course, my mother wasn't having that shit. Her ass didn't want to take care of me, let alone a grandchild, so she took me to the clinic once I told her I was pregnant by a boy from school. I couldn't tell her the truth.

At the clinic, the nurse said I couldn't get an abortion because I was too far along and four months later, I gave birth to a baby boy that I named Kamari. My mother passed him off to my aunt and she had been raising him as her son. When I found out Zuri's father had been raping her over and over again, if you could call it that, my hate for her increased tremendously. It often made me wonder if she knew about us all along and didn't say anything.

Zuri's dad was the reason I let these men come and go in my life and in my bed, and I hated that bitch for not knowing what happened to me in her own home. It didn't matter that I agreed to do it and over time, enjoyed it and looked forward to fucking him when I went over there. Daman was fine, so that made it easier to deal with.

After Jeff left, I scrolled through my phone and found the video of me and Zuri's ex-boyfriend, Kevin, having sex. The two of them dated for a while after Daman went to prison. Kevin was so in love with her and it made me sick, because I had him first. We met one night at the bar and we were so drunk, it was ridiculous. I took him back to my place and he didn't realize what was going on. I never thought the video would come in handy, but clearly it did. I opened the text message box up under Zuri's name and attached the file. I pressed send and waited for her to respond.

***

Zuri

The next morning, I woke up next to Brick and I had to admit, I was happy to have him back in my life. All he had to do was keep his promise and I was willing to make our new relationship work. I got up from the bed and grabbed my cellphone, so I could text Jason and see how he was doing, and apologize again for the crazy shit Brick did to him. The first thing I saw was a text from nasty-ass Kyra. Apparently, she sent me a video. I wasn't going to look at it, because I wanted nothing to do with her, but I was curious to know what the hell this bitch was sending me. I waited until I got into the bathroom to open it up and pressed play. The quality of the footage wasn't that great, but I wasn't blind either. There were two naked bodies, so I flipped the phone sideways to see it full screen. It was a video of her and my ex, Kevin, having sex.

I texted the video to his trifling ass with the quickness. The whole time we were together, he gave me grief about being in a committed relationship with him and having ho'-ass Kyra as a best friend, but he had the nerve to fuck her. These niggas wasn't loyal these days.

Three minutes later, this man was blowing my phone up, but I didn't answer because I didn't want Brick to hear my conversation. After I used the bathroom, I peeked inside the room to make sure Brick was still asleep. His sexy, looney-tune ass was still knocked out, so I snuck downstairs and went outside. The last thing I wanted was for him to wake up and catch me on the phone with another dude. He already proved he could be a deranged man on more than one occasion. When he said he was fucked up about me I felt that shit, but insane as it may sound, I was fucked up about him too.

Gently closing the door, I went and stood by the garage door in case he came looking for me and called him back. It was like he was waiting on my call. His ass answered on the first damn ring.

"Zuri?"

"What?"

"What the hell did you just send me?" He was acting dumb like he didn't recognize who he was looking at.

"Gee, I don't know Kevin, why don't you tell me? I mean, you are the porn star on *Candid Camera*."

"Where did you get that from?"

"Oh, I think we both know where this video came from, genius."

"It's not how it looks, I swear it ain't. Just let me explain."

"Kevin," I sighed. "You know, none of that even matters. I've moved on, so that's no longer my concern. I just wanted you to see what she sent me."

"That happened before we even got together. I never knew that you and her were friends. Let's talk about this."

"No, you can go and talk to Kyra. Now, I understand why you didn't want me around her and how you knew she was a whole ho' outchea."

"Will you just stop and listen please? That video is from a long time ago, before we even got together. I met her in this bar one night and we had been drinking. One thing led to another and all I know is, we ended up at her place having sex. I didn't even know she recorded us."

"Oh, well that makes it better." I laughed. "You expect me to believe that shit?"

"I'm telling you the truth. Do you remember that double date we went on?"

"What about it?"

"I told her not to tell you about it, because I wanted to be with you."

"And, you felt like you couldn't tell me that in the beginning?"

"No, if you knew about that we would've never made it that far."

"That whole relationship was built on a lie."

"No, it wasn't and I swear, I never touched that girl again. Can we at least have a sit-down about this? I don't want to lose you as a friend."

"No, why should I? You fucked Kyra."

"I told you that happened before me and you."

"I don't know that."

"If you look at the video again, you will see that I look different from what I look like now. You're a smart girl, figure that shit out. She's just trying to ruin our friendship."

"Well, she succeeded and at this point, we don't have a friendship. I have a new man and he ain't having that, so I'm not doing nothing to jeopardize what we're building."

"So, it's like that now?"

"It's been like this, so I don't know what you speak of. Anyway, I have to go. Goodbye."

I hung up on him and blocked his number. There was nothing else he could ever say to me. As for Kyra, I was gone tag that ass soon, so she better hope her set was up to date. That bitch tried me for the absolute last time. Before I went back inside, I had to keep my promise to Jason and text him. That was the least I could do after letting Brick ruin our night out on the town. When I opened up my messages, I saw that he beat me to it and it made me smile. That meant he wasn't mad at me. He was such a good person and he didn't deserve what cuckoo did to him.

Jason: I hope everything is okay over there. Just checking on you
Zuri: Hey!! Everything is good. I'm so sorry about last night. I had no idea that he would pop up to my house like that. Please don't be mad at me ☹
Jason: Hey, I could never be mad at you
Zuri: So we good?
Jason: Of course we are
Zuri: Okay. I owe you lunch
Jason: I'm holding you to that
Zuri: K. I'll talk to you later
Jason: ☺

Things worked themselves out and I was happy about that. Jason and I were still friends and I finally got my man. For the first time in a long time, I felt like shit was finally about to go my way. With my phone in hand, I was on my way back inside, then my phone started ringing. Me and my big mouth spoke too soon. It was Daman calling. I was so not ready to talk to him, but I was already on a roll, so I might as well handle all my personal affairs.

Heavily sighing into the phone, I answered. "What?"

"What's going on?"

"Nothing, you tell me?"

"What's that supposed to mean?"

There was no point in beating around the bush, so I gave it to him raw and uncut. "So, you mean to tell me that after all those times you told me to stay away from Kyra, it was off the strength that you was fucking her?"

"What'chu talkin' about?" he asked.

Daman was always good at playing the dumb role, like somebody was stupid. The blind role was something I did quite often a while ago, but being stupid was never one of my traits.

"What we not gone do is play dumb. Kyra told me all about you and her sleeping together when we was in the eighth grade, and how it lasted for a year. All I want is confirmation that it's true."

The hesitation is his voice was the only answer I needed. It was always better when it came from the horse's mouth. Besides, I knew it was true, 'cause how else would she know about the birthmark without sucking and fucking the dick? One way or another, it didn't matter. I had Zaddy dick in the house and that shit was like dope. As a matter of fact, I needed another dose, so I was ready to hang up.

"Well, I'm gone. I got shit to do besides listen to a guilty muthafucka breathe into the phone."

"Wait!" Daman shouted and took a deep breath. "I did sleep with her on more than one occasion. I'm not proud of what I did, but you have to forgive me."

My whole head swung around like on *The Exorcist*. "Who have to forgive you? Not I, bruh. You are sadly mistaken."

"Ohhh, so, I'm bruh now? First, I was Father, now I'm bruh. I get it now. You got another nigga beatin' ya back in, so it's fuck me now."

"Nah, you don't get it. For one, I'm grown and I can fuck whoever I want to. For two, you been lying from the jump. How the fuck you was smashing my ex best-friend? That shit is bogus as fuck."

"Who you fuckin'?" he asked boldly.

"That's irrelevant."

"Nah, you have so much to say, so tell me who you fuckin'?"

"You wouldn't know him if I told you."

"I see you acting like yo' mama." He really had me fucked up, 'cause he talked about my mama like a stank-ass dog. She was every bitch, slut and ho' in his book, but he had me fucked up.

"I'll be that, but my new nigga loves the way I suck, lick, slurp and fuck his big-ass dick. He has no complaints, but you know that already."

"You remember this shit when I get out. I'ma fuck you up for talkin' to me like you crazy."

"Oh, you mad, 'cause somebody else fuckin' me better than you? Get the fuck outta here. As a matter of fact, I'm about to go back in the house and get my back beat out right now. I hope you can hear my screams all the way in yo' cell when he bust me wide open."

"Zuri!" he shouted, but I bammed it on his ass.

Click!

Now I was happy as fuck. I went back in the house and got in the bed with my baby. Daman was steadily blowing my phone up, so I did him a favor and answered it, but I didn't say anything. I sat the phone beside the pillow, out of plain sight and let him listen to me ride Brick's big-ass dick. I made sure I was extra loud just in case Daman felt the need to holler into the receiver. That'll teach his ass about trying me and calling me out my name.

Chapter 14

Zuri

Saturday morning, I found myself sitting in the parking lot at the Martin County Correctional Institution at eight o'clock in the morning. The guilt from my actions the other day was literally beating my ass. Regardless of the steps I was taking to get away from Daman, it was hard because my heart was still with him. My conscious was a constant reminder that I needed to end things for good. It was only right. Without a doubt, I loved him and walking away was easier said than done. So, there I sat anxiously waiting to see his face since he wasn't expecting a visit. The last time he saw me in person was six months ago.

There was so much that needed to be said in person and doing it by phone wouldn't suffice. The more I thought about it, the more emotional I became. *How did I end up here? Why couldn't I be normal? Why am I so fucked up?* The entire situation had me despondent and I didn't know if I was coming or going. A gut-wrenching sob tore through my chest followed by my fist meeting the steering wheel. The sound of my horn caught the attention of some passerby's as they headed toward the entrance of the building. My grief poured out in uncontrollable tears and I could no longer contain myself.

"Daman, what did you do to me?" I screamed.

As I clutched the diamond locket around my neck, I sobbed harder. On my tenth birthday, Daman presented it to me and it held sentimental value. The inside read: *My biggest blessing happened the day you were born. I love you.*

The clock on my dashboard appeared blurry in sight due to all my crying, yet it confirmed that fifteen minutes had passed and the registration process had begun. Slowly pulling tissue from my purse beside me, I cleaned the water from my face and blew my nose.

Once I finished giving myself a once over in the mirror, I got out and walked toward the building. Upon my entrance, I was asked a series of questions before walking through the metal detector and finally the physical search. Although it was done by an officer of the same sex, it was still uncomfortable, which was why I hated to visit.

By the time I was violated in every aspect of the word, visitation had begun and I was able to go into the visiting park and wait on Daman to come out.

My ass was a nervous wreck as I sat and waited in seventy-five-degree weather. The sun wasn't beaming just yet, but I knew it was coming eventually. My hands trembled terribly underneath the table, so I placed them between my legs in an effort to cease the movement. It was hard to relax at that point.

A few minutes later, I spotted Daman coming through the door with a bewildered look on his face. He probably didn't want to see me after that stunt I pulled.

Daman's eyes roamed the yard, so I stood up so he could see me. The moment he laid eyes on me, a frown instantly appeared as he shook his head from side to side. At times he could be hard to read, so there was no telling what was going through his mind. He walked up to the picnic table and sat down across from me without speaking to me.

Daman simply folded his arms across his chest, eyeing me with a blank stare. His expression alone was confirmation that this visit was going to be less than pleasant. Maybe visiting him was a mistake after all, but I was there and it was a little too late to turn back.

"Hi, Daman. How are you?" He didn't respond. Hell, he didn't blink either, his face hardened in anger. "Are you going to say something?"

Daman's jaw tightened. "Don't you have a dick that you could be riding right about now instead of fuckin' with me?"

My head instantly dropped in shame. "I'm sorry." I whispered.

"Don't bother apologizing. You meant to do that foul ass shit," he snapped. "That's what you out there doing acting like a ho'?"

"No." My eyes met his and I snapped back. "I only did it to make you mad because of what you did to me. How do you think I felt when I heard about you fucking Kyra? You have no idea."

"So, you fuckin' a nigga while I was on the phone made you feel better about the situation?" He placed both hands on the table and leaned forward. "That shit was flat out disrespectful. You lucky I'm worried about my operation in here 'cause I'll slap the fuck outta you for trying me like I'm some pussy ass nigga."

Daman pointed his index finger in my direction. "I'm gettin' out one day so keep that shit in mind."

The sound of his teeth grinding made my skin crawl and my ears ache. "Zuri, you so fuckin' lucky I can't afford to go to the solitary confinement 'cause I swear to God I'll fuck you up right now on this yard."

My father never threatened me like that in life and it had me concerned. Because as a child and teenager, he never beat me or my siblings often. It had to be really bad for us to get a whooping. It took no effort for me to produce tears and turn this thing back around on him. Daman was nothing like Brick, he hated to see me cry. The minute the tears slid down my cheeks he looked away.

"Whose fault is it that I'm like this anyway? Yours." My bottom lip trembled. "You are the reason I'm fucked up right now. All these years you had me thinking that what we were doing was okay and it wasn't. You knew better and did nothing to fix it." My voice raised bringing unwanted attention in our direction. "This is all your fault."

Daman placed his eyes back on me. "Keep your voice down before they come over here. The last thing I need is for them to come over here messing up our visitation."

"I'm not staying long anyway." I played with my fingers under the table. "I came here because I need closure and in order to do that I need to know how could you molest me and brainwash me into thinking it was okay."

Daman was silent for a while. Then he reached over toward me with his palms up. At first, I hesitated, but eventually I placed my hands into his. My heart sped up, as I anticipated his next words.

"Zuri, you're my daughter and you know I would never hurt you intentionally. The things we shared was out of love. Everything I did with you was because I love you and that's what two people do when they're in love."

"But you're my father. How is that right?"

"I love you and I brought you into this world, so I don't see anything wrong with me loving you physically. I've never abused you sexually and I didn't force you to do anything you didn't want to do. That is what you call rape and molestation. We had consensual sex. That was something we agreed upon. Our moments were special and we made beautiful music, so don't let anyone tell you differently."

150

Daman closed his eyes and released a long-winded sigh before opening them. "No one on the outside knows how I feel about you. We are the only ones that understands our bond and that's all that matters. It's always been us against the world and you know that. They want to see us apart."

My heart panged with guilt because I did love him and I agreed with the things he said. But that didn't remove the fact that what we did was wrong. My throat tightened as I tried to keep my composure and not show emotion.

"What we did was wrong and that's not the way a father should love his daughter." Gently pulling my hand from the grips of his hot palms, I proceeded to make my point. "I'm a counselor that deals with this type of thing and it's wrong on every level. It also makes me a hypocrite because I'm engaging in the very thing I stand against at work."

"I understand what you're saying just hear me out, though. One day I fell on my knees and asked God to take away my desire for you, just rip that shit right out of my heart." I could hear the tears in his voice although none ran down his face. "But God told me that He gave you to me to love how you should be loved. So, that's what I did, and that's what I'll always do. Unless you no longer want that love. If that's how it is, go ahead and crush my mutha-fuckin' heart."

He stared at me with puppy dog eyes and with a vul-nerability that I never associated with him because of strength.

"I don't know what to say about God telling you to love me in that way."

Daman rubbed his forehead in frustration. "So, what are you saying? Everything we built over the years is over?" He took a deep breath. "Just like that, huh?"

"This is not easy for me. I still love you, but I'm battling with what's right and wrong."

"All I wanted was for us to be together, but if you feel like it's wrong, then you can get up and walk away for good. I promise I won't stop you. If you want me to rot in this prison cell, I'll do that for you. Your happiness means the world to me and I'll do whatever you want me to do. Just say the word."

Without looking at him, I slid from the bench fully prepared to make my final exit.

"Remember that I will always love you and no one will ever compare to what we had. You can have everything. The house and the money. It means nothing without you, so I don't need it."

My back was turned to him, so he couldn't see the tears cascading down my face. It didn't matter who was watching because they couldn't feel or even begin to understand my pain. I stood there in silence for a minute contemplating my next move. My heart was telling me to stay, but my mind was telling me to leave. No longer able to fight it, I turned around and walked into his strong arms. With my head buried in his chest, I sobbed like he was on death row and on his way to be executed.

"Don't cry, baby, I'm here for you. Always have been, always will be. It ain't a nigga walking that's gon' do the shit I do for you and he damn sure ain't gon' love you the way I do."

I nodded my head in agreement.

Daman had a hold on me that I just couldn't shake. One minute I was ready to leave him and the next I was in his arms crying my eyes out. His words sucked me right back in like a vacuum and it felt like there was no escape. Our relationship was wrong on so many levels, but how could I just up and leave my first love? The man that meant the world to me with no consideration to his feelings, especially when I knew for a fact he loved me.

Chapter 15

Gucci

One Month Later

Things between me and Mehzani were going above and beyond my expectations. It seemed as if she had kicked her addiction completely. I took her to enroll into school, so she could start her road to redemption.

She wanted to be a pharmacist, a legal one. With only one year up under her belt, she needed three more years before she could enroll into the pharmacy program. She attended FAMU, but couldn't get her credits transferred until she paid a balance of six thousand dollars. I paid that for her, so she could register with Nova Southeastern University. Mehzani didn't want to go far, but I told her she needed to get out of her comfort zone and be around people she didn't know. Needless to say, she would be local and I would have to keep an eye out for her. However, something in my gut said I didn't need to worry too much about her going backwards as long as she had me.

In between time, I let her know the real reason why we couldn't have unprotected sex. She was cool with it and respected my honesty. Since she didn't have anything to hide, I took her to the clinic to get a complete examination. I had never put so much time, effort and commitment into a woman before and it felt damn good. Well, there was one female that came close, but greed and betrayal tore us apart. That was another story though.

I could see things going far in me and Mehzani's relationship, since we decided to make it official. At first, she was reluctant out of fear that I only saw her as a charity case, a project. It took a while for her to let her guard down and when that day came, I made a promise to never hurt her.

Ever since then, I have showed her what a real man looks like. Of course, there were some haters on the sidelines, but that was to be expected. I didn't give a damn what nobody had to say, because no one paid my bills. One day, I ran into one of my old ho's and she was thirty-eight hot. She said, word on the street was that I wifed up a flakka head. That ho' was just mad, because all she got was hard dick and bubble gum. The bitch was fine, but her head was empty. I couldn't do shit with a bad bitch, who had an eighth-grade education.

In due time, every bitch I used to fuck with, who had something to say about Mehzani, was about to hate her even more. I was about to grab my baby something fresh off the lot, her choice of course. My beliefs were that a man should never give another female a reason to laugh at his main lady. The main lady should be laughing at his old ho's.

"Bae," Mehzani yelled from the kitchen. "Do you want ice?"

"Yeah."

Mehzani walked into the room, wearing those Victoria's Secret PINK shorts I like. She knew those were to only be worn around the house. My eyes locked into those beautiful brown eyes of hers. They were so tantalizing and I could get lost in them forever. That always made her blush when I looked at her.

"Why are you looking at me like that?" Her cheeks sat up high.

"I'm happy you're here with me."

"So am I." Mehzani smiled and handed me the glass she was holding.

"Are you really?"

"Of course, why wouldn't I be? You saved my life and I owe you that. You didn't use me for sex and you didn't rush me. You allowed me to make the first move. I've never had that before."

I leaned closer to her and held her hand. "I think that's the other way around, you saved me. You slowed me down and turned me into a better man, one that cares about a woman's feelings. I was hard on these ho's out here and now they're jealous, because you have what they wanted from me." I placed my hand over my heart to give her a visual. "This was cold before I met you and I don't care about your past, because I have one too. All I care about is your future."

And, just like that, I had her in tears. My touching message fucked her mind with my words. I knew she was locked in and no one, I mean no one, could take me away from her.

***

Deja

I never thought being a mother would be such a hard job. Sometimes I felt as if I gave up my life and independence to become a stay-at-home mom. Six years ago, I met Brick after I walked away from my abusive ex on a forever note. He came into my life during my darkest hours and made me love again. After a romantic whirlwind of only five months, I got pregnant with our first child, Breanna.

From the moment I told him we were expecting, Brick stepped up and made me quit my job at the doctor's office.

At first, I was against it but I really did love him, so I did whatever he told me to do. Besides, he was very persuasive, yet demanding. Brick was the type of dude that needed to be in control of every aspect of your life, but it came with the guarantee of being taken care of at all times. The added bonus was he wasn't stingy and he didn't clock the money he gave me. As long as I listened to him, everything was perfect, but I remember one of the times I disobeyed his order and stayed out past my curfew.

"Girl, it's only midnight and we ain't ready to go yet. Brandon will be okay with the baby for another two hours," Crystal insisted.

"No. I have to go." I nervously bit my nails, staring at the watch he bought me. "You just don't understand."

"He ain't that damn bad. He knows you just had a baby three months ago and you miss going out."

Obviously, she didn't know Brick, because he was just that bad when it came down to obeying him. But, since I had been drinking, I let it go and figured he would be okay since I had been confined to the house during my entire pregnancy.

"Okay, but if I get in trouble, I'm blaming you. And, I need to at least be home by one." I decided to relax and enjoy the party for another hour.

"Okay, I got 'chu."

Thirty minutes later, Brick walked into the yard, carrying our daughter in his arms and he had the nastiest look on his face. Immediately, I jumped to my feet and scurried towards him to keep him from causing a scene and embarrassing me in front of Crystal's family that threw the party.

"B-bae, what you doing here?" I stuttered.

"I should be asking you the same thing."

"I was just about to leave." That lie rolled off with the quickness.

"You look mighty damn comfortable for a person that was on the way out." By this time, people were looking in our direction, but I ignored them and tried to walk past him.

"Please, don't do this here," I begged.

"Fuck that, you think I give a fuck about these people? I told you to be home at midnight like muthafuckin' Cinderella. What the fuck you think I bought you a watch for?"

Brick handed me the baby. "You must've forgot you have a new baby and have no business out this time of night. You got me fucked up, let's go."

Crystal finally spoke up. "Don't do her like that. Ain't nobody here but my family and we just having fun."

"I don't give a fuck about who here, 'cause she ain't stupid enough to cheat when she got it made. None of these niggas in attendance ain't got shit on me."

Brick escorted me off the premises and to the car. The entire car ride had me scared, out of fear of what he was going to do to me. I just hoped he didn't put his hands on me.

As soon as we got into the house, he snapped. "The next time I give yo' ass a curfew, you better slip in this bitch like Cinderella and I ain't playin' wit' yo ass." He tossed his keys on the table. "I'ma teach you about being disrespectful. Put the baby down."

Right off the bat I started crying. Heavy tears rolled down my face as I clutched our baby tight in my arms. My legs wouldn't be still for nothing in the world. It looked as if I had to pee. "Brick, please. I'm sorry. You promised you wouldn't hit me."

"Put the baby down and I'm not gone say it no mo'."

"Please. I'm sorry."

"I'm counting to three and my baby better be out yo' muthafuckin' arms." He paused. "One."

My first mind said, don't test him. I knew it was coming, because he wanted me to put Breanna down badly. Instead of battling with him, I laid Breanna down in her playpen. My heart was beating so hard, my throat was vibrating just standing there.

"Brick, you promised you would never hit me again. Please don't. I'm begging you." He wasn't abusive to me physically, but one time he did hit me out of anger and promised to never do it again. Up until now, he kept that promise.

He was standing by the couch looking at me sideways and grinding his teeth. "Come here."

"No please." I shook my head.

"Deja, come here now."

"Are you going to hit me?"

"If I have to come to you, I will."

Deep down, I felt like he wasn't going to hit me, so I took slow steps towards him. "I'm sorry. I'll never do it again, I promise."

"Oh, I know that." He reached underneath the table, pulled out two dictionaries and handed them to me.

"What am I supposed to do with these?"

"Go stand in the corner and put 'em on your head and don't move until I tell you to."

Brick made me stand in that corner for a total of two hours, knees buckling and all.

There was a point in time I always had thoughts of us being together forever, but then he caught a case and ended up with a five-year bid. It was funny how the judge broke us up and changed all of that.

I stood by his side for the first year and shortly after, I was mentally drained. He was too demanding and I couldn't picture myself going through that for an additional four years. It took me weeks to plan for my final visitation with him. I had to get my thoughts together and stand firm on my decision, even if he begged me to stay. When I broke the news to him, he wasn't happy, but my happiness was much more important.

Brick was everything I wanted and needed in a man. He was a boss and he handled his business and his home. My days were mostly spent in the house, performing wife duties. I cooked, cleaned, and washed his dirty clothes, while he was out working the streets. He had turned me into an old maid and I was only twenty-six. Speaking of the devil, I had my own situation and it couldn't wait. So, I picked up the phone and called the one person who was going to help me get through it.

"Hello." Gucci picked up on the fourth ring.

"We need to talk."

"About what?" he asked.

"Brick."

"Oh," he hesitated. "Um. Okay."

"When can you come over?"

"I'll come through tomorrow."

"Okay." I hung up the phone and started strategizing.

Destiny Skai

Chapter 16

Brick

"So, what's the word on Legend?" I stood in front of my crew irritated, with my arms folded across my chest. I had a mission to accomplish and these niggas was round here fuckin' off. "It's been a whole muthafuckin' month and I haven't heard shit yet. Ain't nobody workin', huh?"

The room was silent.

I inched my way closer to the desk and placed my palms down on it. "Please, don't speak at once. I wanna hear all y'all." They knew my sarcasm meant I was serious and pissed off. There were three things I didn't play about and that was business, money, and my woman. Everyone in that room was well aware of my reputation, so that spoke for itself. "When I talk, I expect muthafuckin' answers. You think I'm just standing up here talkin' for my health?"

Coop sat up in his seat to answer his question. "The last I heard was the nigga took flight to Texas a few weeks ago and he ain't been seen since."

I punched the table with my hand. "That's what the fuck I'm talm 'bout. Some muthafuckin' results. I done got rid of Playa already, so if I have to eliminate these last two niggas myself, what the fuck I need y'all for?"

They all appeared to be nervous as they looked in my direction. Their eyes were on me, but they couldn't look me directly in the eyes, except for one youngin' in particular and his name was Skeet. He was the hungriest in the bunch and possibly the most vicious.

"A few minutes ago, every last one of y'all was joking and playin'. Now it's time to get down to business, and the cat got y'all muthafuckin' tongues. Y'all niggas act like y'all just got caught lettin' a smoker suck ya dick."

Coop busted out laughing. "Bruh, you stupid as fuck. You got these niggas scared to answer you."

Coop was my ace, my right-hand man and the realest nigga in my camp. We met during my teenage years when I was running the streets. When I caught the bid for five years, he held me down without me having to ask. He stood in the paint like a G and that was why I considered him my brother from another mother.

"I don't give a fuck about that. This is a grown man's business." I hit the table again. "If you wanna play games, take ya ass back to little league, or get 'cha ass back on the porch." I stretched my arms out at an even level to my shoulders.

"This is my organization and I'll die 'bout this shit. I need goons behind me ready to bust they guns."

I dropped my arms and eyed every last one of them evenly.

"If you ain't ready, get the fuck up out my seat and exit stage left. I don't need nan muthafucka here taking up space and I can't depend on them. If you ain't 'bout BMB, stop wasting my muthafuckin' time, real talk."

Skeet stood up and faced me. "With all due respect, Ion know 'bout nobody else in here, but I been lookin' for his ass high and low. I'm wit'cha all the way, believe dat. I'm built for this shit and you know I'm rockin' wit'cha until the wheels fall off the whip." The lil' nigga was hyped.

"That's good to hear, youngin', and believe that I pay attention to detail. But rule number one is to remain seated during my meetings, unless instructed otherwise. Now, like I was saying, don't shit go unnoticed around here. You other niggas need to take notes, 'cause I got eyes every-where."

"Pay attention to this young nigga," Tone finally spoke up. "Man, you must be crazy."

Tone was an older dude I was in prison with and he often needed a reminder of who ran shit. "You must be crazy if you think you run shit. If I say take notes, then that's what I mean. BMB is all me." I hit my chest like King Kong. "And, don't forget it. Ion give a fuck how old you are and that you stuck in yo' ways. Nigga, I'm stuck in mine too. Tighten up and do some goddamn work, 'cause Ion see Beyoncé up in this bitch, so none of you muthafuckas irre-placeable."

His lips were pulled tight, while he nodded his head. All I knew is that his next words better be spoken wisely, 'cause I'll clap his ass right here with no remorse. "Got it, boss," he replied.

"Good." I smirked. "And, don't you forget it."

"Got'cha."

"Oh, I know and I'm gon' make sure you don't." I look over at Coop. "Bruh, gimme the supplies." My ace handed me a notebook and a pen, then I handed it to Tone. He was reluctant as he took it from my hand. "Write two hundred times, I will follow Brick's rules."

Tone looked at me in disbelief. "Bruh, you serious?"

"As a heart attack." The tools my mom used to disci-pline me came in handy. She never put her hands on me. Instead, she used techniques to break me in other ways. So, as an adult, I adapted her techniques in my relationships and business dealings. Grown people hated to be treated like or referred to as children and it always straightened out their behavior.

"Can I just get a whooping instead?" I asked, as she made me write five hundred times that I will behave in school.

"No, son. A beating is too easy and it will be over in less than five minutes. You will learn in life that you don't have to put your hands-on people to make them obey you." She stood beside me with her hands on her hips, watching me write.

"This weekend and the remainder of the month, we will be at the park, so you can pick up trash. I'm not raising no dummy, Brandon, and you will learn how to behave. There is no room in white America for a black man." She leaned down and kissed me on the cheek. "Even if I have to work the black off of you. I love you, son, and one day you will appreciate everything I've done to help you."

My attention was back on the group as a whole. "If anybody in here don't like my rules, feel free to exit the building now." No one moved.

***

The day for me to meet the distributer finally came into play. So, Gucci was safe for now.

We walked inside a strip club that housed nothing but Spanish chicks and a few thick white ones. Cosmetic surgery did them some justice because they were stacked nicely. The security guard escorted us to what I assumed was the VIP section, draped with red curtains.

"They here, Boss."

"Thanks, Sergio." He extended his hand for both of us to shake. "Nice to meet you, Brick. Have a seat." He looked at Gucci for confirmation. "This is Brick, right?"

"Yeah."

Gucci and I got comfy on the cushioned seats.

"What's going on, Coop?"

"I'll have that ready for you in a few days." Coop leaned forward and fixed himself a drink.

Hector had a smirk on his face. "So, Brick, I hear you need a plug?"

"You heard correct." I replied with a smug look on my face.

"Have you heard of the Riccardo Cartel?"

"Yeah, I heard a l'il something."

"Good." He nodded his head. "So, you know that we don't play and we serious when it comes down to business?"

"Yeah, I heard." I leaned forward and folded my hands together. I looked him dead in the eyes, so he would know that I wasn't shit to play with. I didn't give a fuck what his last name was or what cartel he was with.

"I've heard about you just like you've heard about me. I take my business serious and I don't play games when it comes down to my money."

Hector's lips were pressed firmly together, as he nodded his head up and down. He then pointed his finger in my direction. "I like you and I think I'm going to enjoy doing business with you."

"You won't regret it." I assured him.

Gucci and I sat across from Hector and discussed the shipment that would make me a very rich man in the next few months. All my crew had to do was push that shit like they life was hanging in the balance. I was gone make sure everything was straight anyway. Being a hustler came naturally to me and embedded deep in my bloodstream. As a teenager, I had to get it from the muscle after my old girl departed this earth. Hector's mouth was moving, but all I could hear was my mother's voice.

"Baby, family will stab you in the back every chance they get. Your most loyal people will be the ones that don't share the same DNA. Be careful who you keep around you. Mama won't always be around to protect you from this cold world."

My eyes shot in Gucci's direction then back to Hector. He was babbling about some wild parties and threesomes he had with multiple chicks. "Can you help with that, Brick? You seem like a player with a lot of bad females on your trail."

"What you looking for? I know a lot of females, but not prostitutes or no shit like that."

"I want some nice shit." He sat up and grinned hard, like he was looking at a bad bitch right then. "Nice eye candy when I go out. Hook that up and I'll pay you for every female you bring to me."

"Y'all niggas serious right now?" Gucci jumped in and his tone was less than pleasant, but I didn't give a fuck.

"Nigga, hush when you hear two bosses discussing business. Fuck wrong wit' 'chu? You working for the Save a Ho' Foundation?"

"Whateva, nigga. We supposed to be discussing this work, not selling ho's."

"Nigga, I want money from every corner and avenue." I eyed him hard. "I want my cash from dope and ho's. I don't give a fuck." My focus was back on this Colombian muthafucka with the mountain of money. "This nigga trippin'."

Hector had my attention. I never saw myself as a pimp or no shit like that, but if the price was right, I'd bring him a bus load of ho's. Scratching my chin, I smiled like the Grinch. "How much you talkin'?"

"I'll pay you fifteen hundred a chick." He tossed that number with little thought, so I knew this wasn't his first rodeo.

"Oh yeah, I'ma make this shit shake. I gotchu."

"Bad shit, Brick."

"Nigga, what the fuck I look like bringing you a booger wolf? I got this."

Hector cracked up. "What the fuck is a booger wolf?"

"A beastly-looking bitch." I laughed. "I'm sure you done ran into a few of them on occasions."

"Yeah, don't bring those over here."

"Look at me. I'm a boss. I only fuck with hot shit."

"Good." He extended his hand. "We have a deal."

We shook hands.

"Fa'sho."

Hector picked up a cigar, cut the top off and handed it to me. "This is an exclusive Irish Whiskey." He handed one to Gucci as well.

"To a new business venture." Hector lit them and we all took a puff. The hit was sweet. "Try this." He pulled out a bottle of some shit I never seen before.

"What's that?" Gucci asked.

"Aguardiente." His accent was thick as hell.

"What the hell is that?" I repeated.

"A Cristal. It's twenty-nine percent alcohol from Columbia."

We sat with Hector for another hour, while sipping on that exclusive shit. Hector was trying to get a nigga fucked up. That was cool with me. My work for the day was done, so I was about to go home and fuck the shit outta Zuri. Her ass was about to be climbing the walls like Spiderman.

"We out, man. I'm fucked up and I need my girl right about now."

Hector laughed and his eyes shrunk. "I can dig it."

Gucci and I got up and dapped him up, then cleared it. My mind was on Zuri's sexy ass and I could feel my shit throbbing, but I needed my brain to send signals to stop until I made it to her. A nigga ain't need to be getting rocked up around other niggas.

Chapter 17

Zuri

Since the day I left visitation, my head and heart had been all over the place. One minute, I wanted to be with Daman, and the next, I wanted to block him from my life for good. At times, I felt like the devil was truly riding my back. Each day that I spent with Brick, he made me want to be a better woman. When Daman said that God told him to love me the way I needed to be loved I believed him at that moment, but now I wasn't too sure. How could God give him such a message if that was a sin? Now I wasn't a holy roller, nor could I really identify myself as a Christian, but I knew that incest went on in the bible. It didn't make it right, but it was there.

To say my transition was going to be easy would be a lie. Truth is, Daman was all I had, so I knew letting go wouldn't be easy. However, Brandon Riccardo came into my life at the perfect time to help me push past the pain that I was guaranteed to experience. Just the thought alone made chest tight. There was no telling how things would play out if he wasn't by my side. I probably would be in the insane asylum or the county jail. Either way, I'm grateful to have him in my life.

Brick kept his promise and made my happiness his number-one priority, aside from his business. I told him business was first and I wouldn't bitch about it, as long as it didn't require him to forget about me. He promised to take care of home and be faithful. That made me blush, knowing he would make loving him easy, but I knew it was easier said than done. My previous relationships made me jealous and I'm not afraid to admit it, but Daman really did a number on me when he cheated on me with Kyra. Now, he was the reason I had trust issues. It wasn't Brick's fault, because he hasn't given me a reason to doubt him, so I had to try my best and keep my insecurities in check.

Brick stood on the side of the bed getting dressed. My eyes were wide ass open, like I'd never seen what he had to offer. That happened every time he was in my presence. "Gawd, why you so fine?" I licked my lips seductively.

Every time he smiled, his eyes had this glow in them. "The same reason you fine." He licked his lips.

"Yeah, but I'm not fine as you."

"You fine to me and that's all that matters." He pulled his tank top over his head. "And, we both fine when we laying down."

"I'm not playing with you." I sat up on the edge of the bed, allowing my legs to swing freely. "How long will you be gone today?"

"I don't know. A few hours, why, what's up?" He sat down on the bed and put on his shoes, one by one.

"I was going to cook us some dinner."

Bricked stopped in the middle of tying his shoes and looked out the corner of his eye. "Damn, bae, you trying to kill me already? We ain't even past the probationary stage in our relationship yet and you wanna take a nigga out his misery."

His laughter was so hearty and contagious, I couldn't help but join in. "Why you dissing my cooking though? You ate it this morning."

Brick finished putting on both of his shoes and stood up. "That's breakfast food, baby. It's hard to mess that up."

"Okay." I folded my arms across my chest. "You gone be hungry tonight."

"No, I won't. It's something in here that I can eat." He licked those soft pink lips of his seductively.

"You so nasty."

"Nah, you nasty, 'cause I didn't say what it was."

"Then why you licked your lips?"

"That's what I do, baby. I'm a freak and this will get me full right here." Brick rubbed his hand between my legs and bit down on my neck, forcing me to clutch my pearls.

I clamped my thighs on his hand. "Stop before you start something you can't finish and you miss your meeting."

"Yeah, let me stop." He backed away, pulling his hand back. "What you gone be doing while I'm gone?"

"I'll probably catch up on my reading, since I don't have to cook and kill you tonight." My inner petty kicked in and I stuck my tongue out. Brick leaned in, catching my tongue with his teeth and tongued me down. Damn, he could kiss. That's all I needed to get me started. I reached for his belt buckle, but he grabbed my hands to stop me.

"Bae, I gotta go."

"Well, quit teasing me."

"I'm sorry."

Brick reached in his pocket and pulled out a wad of cash. Peeling off three one-hundred-dollar bills, he placed them in my hand. "Go to the spa and get a massage or something. I need you loose and relaxed when I get back, so we can try some new shit in the bedroom."

"I like the sound of that."

"Good. I'll be back later on this evening. Keep it tight for me." He gave me a pop kiss and left.

Brick must've read my mind, because I was due for my bi-monthly spa treatment anyway. I got up and got dressed quickly, before heading out.

One my way there, I stopped at the corner store and when I came out, Kyra was standing on the sidewalk. I had been waiting for this day to present itself for a while. A part of me didn't want to fight her, because I was done with Daman, but the other part of me needed to beat her ass to let her know shit wasn't sweet. That argument confirmed she had always been a close enemy of mine.

In order to settle the score, I decided today was the day I would dig in that ass. I didn't say one word to her. I just walked up to her and punched her dead in the mouth, leaving her with no choice but to fight back. I was going in on that ho'. She tried to lock up with me when she grabbed my hair, but that wasn't happening. I wrapped her hair around my hand and pounded her face with blow after blow. I could hear a crowd around us, yelling for someone to break it up. Then, someone tried to pull her hair from my hand, but my grip was too tight.

"Break this shit up. I thought y'all were friends," this dude we went to school with yelled.

"Fuck that ho'. She ain't my friend." They were finally able to separate us and I got a good look at her face. That shit was ugly and bloody. "I bet you'll keep your mouth and legs closed next time, bitch."

"Fuck you, ho', you just mad 'cause you thought you was the only one fuckin' that nigga. Ha-ha, bitch, I was fucking him too."

People were standing around with their phones in their hands, so I knew what that meant. This fight was going on Facebook.

Kyra was yelling out all types of shit. "You better watch your back, bitch."

"I don't have to do shit. Ion fear no bitch, so it's whatever, whenever and with whoever. You know about these hands, pussy ho'."

I got in my car and pulled off.

***

Kyra

Seeing myself get beat up on Facebook really pissed me off, but it was okay, because I put that bitch's business on full blast. I couldn't call Kevin to tell him what was going on, because he wasn't too fond of me anymore. For some apparent reason, he always felt like I was a bad influence on Zuri, as if I could make her sleep around. That ho' lucky I couldn't reach out to Brick personally, 'cause I would make him leave her ass with all the dirt I had on her. Instead, I put it on the 'Book to make sure Lauderdale saw it. I knew someone would relay the message.

After the fight, I saw Gucci standing there and that was why I shouted out the reason for us fighting. He would definitely tell Brick all about it. That would teach her ass a valuable lesson. Zuri always had it all with whoever she was messing with and I hated to admit it, but I was vexed about that. My goal was to make sure she lost whatever it was he was trying to build with her. Oh yeah, I was about to dismantle their whole relationship.

I'm certain she thought this thing was over between us, but she had another think coming. This was only the beginning and far from over. I was about to ruin her innocent reputation. Once upon a time, we were best friends, but that changed. Truth is, I couldn't stand her ass. Zuri thought she was God's gift to men. She also thought she was better than me.

Before her and Kevin hooked up, we had already fucked. I knew him from around the way and I already had my eyes on him. It took me a minute to approach him, because the timing wasn't right. He was always with a group of niggas and I was waiting to catch him solo.

I finally caught up with him when we just so happened to be at the same bar. Well, I followed him there, but he didn't know that. We ended up talking, drinking and taking shot after shot. By the end of the night, we were roasted and I took him back to my place. And, I can honestly say I wasn't disappointed. Weeks had gone by and I had not heard from Kevin since the night we had sex.

Then lo and behold, Zuri pops up and tells me how she met some nigga she was falling for quickly. She set up a double date to give us a chance to meet and when we met, I was speechless. Kevin was the mystery man that swept her off her feet.

During dinner, Zuri and my date went to the restroom, leaving me and Kevin at the table. As soon as the coast was clear, he looked at me and said, *"Please don't tell Zuri what happened between us."*

I looked at him like he had smoked some crack. Needless to say, I never said anything. Now, it was a new day and years later, I couldn't wait to tell her about us. I wish I could've seen her face when I dropped that bomb on her.

"Damn, Kyra. Girl, I heard about the fight between you and your bestie." Tasha laughed, as she walked up and sat beside me on my porch.

"Shut the fuck up. That shit only all over Facebook." That bitch got on my nerves. Always talking shit like somebody asked her anything.

She rolled her eyes hard. "Why I got to shut up? It ain't my fault you got beat up."

"That's okay, 'cause believe me when I say this shit ain't over yet," I reassured her.

"What you gone do? 'Cause everybody in Lauderdale talking about that shit."

"So what, let those bitches talk. I bet one of those ho's won't run up." People swore up and down that if you lose one fight, you can't redeem yourself.

"I don't think you're in the best position to be talking shit right about now. Everybody knows you lost and nobody is scared of you."

I rolled my eyes, because Tasha was getting on my damn nerves. This ho' was always in a bitch business with her nosey ass. It was too early in the day for the bullshit.

"When was the last time you beat a bitch ass?" Tasha was silent. "That's what I thought. Now, pass the blunt before I make your ass go home."

Tasha was one of my neighbors and we had been cool for a while now, but her mouth was real slick at times. I took a puff of the blunt and exhaled slowly.

"I am going to ruin that bitch and you can bet that."

"What y'all beefing for anyway?"

"She mad because I fucked her ex-boyfriend and her daddy and I didn't tell her."

"Really, bitch?" Tasha acted surprised.

"Yep. I fucked them good, too."

Tasha shook her head. "That's fucked up. Now I see why she beat your ass."

"Fuck that ho'. I had him first."

"Remind me not to bring my man around you." Tasha laughed, but I could tell when a bitch was being phony.

"Girl, please, your man is ugly and nobody wants him but you." She rolled her eyes. I knew that would shut her ugly ass up.

Tasha thought she was cute because she was red, but truth be told, that ho' looked like a lizard. I wasn't about to let her fuck up my high, so I just kicked back and kept smoking. That weed had me thinking heavy and I came up with the most brilliant idea that would ruin her happy home for good.

My plan was so evil and I couldn't wait to execute it. I was bringing down the house with this one. The things I was about to expose would definitely make her commit suicide. *Maybe that's a good thing though.* When I was done humiliating her, Broward County was going to know her name, along with every other county and state that logged into Facebook and shared my story. The petty book loved gossip and drama and I was about to deliver the hot tea better than Wendy Williams.

Chapter 18

Brick

After the meeting with the squad, I felt like shit was about to take off for me. I had two muthafuckas still in the way, but Skeet had just delivered the news that Legend was back. Apparently, his birthday was in two days and he was throwing this big-ass party. He better enjoy that shit to fullest, 'cause that would be his very last party here in the flesh. The only other parties he gone have is with the Lord or Lucifer, depending on the trip he was about to take.

My ass was walking fast as fuck to my car, so I could get to my queen. I picked up some sex toys and flavored lubes for me and my baby to try tonight. It was time to get her all the way out her shell and introduce her to some freaky shit. Zuri was slightly comfortable, but I wanted more. She had to be buck wild with me in order to keep me interested.

"Aye, Brick," Gucci shouted from behind me. I stopped walking and turned around.

"What's up?"

"I need to show you something real quick." He handed me his phone.

"What is it?" He had me skeptical as fuck.

"Watch this video."

"I don't wanna see shit on Facebook." I tried to hand it back to him, but he wouldn't take it.

"Nah, you wanna see this, bruh."

Without further ado, I watched the video in silence and froze when I stumbled upon a familiar body and outfit.

"Who she fighting?" Deep down in my gut, I had a feeling I knew who the other female was.

"Kyra. I heard they was fighting 'cause they was sleeping wit' the same nigga."

"Well, it ain't me, so she gotta straighten me 'bout this shit." I passed the phone back.

"It's something else too. I don't know what the fuck happened wit' them, but Kyra putting all her business out there."

Gucci showed me a post stating Zuri was fucking her daddy and wouldn't testify in court. The way it was written, it was like she was down with the shit. My head was fucked up after reading that shit.

"Don't show me shit else. I'm 'bout to go handle this right now. I'll holla at 'chu later."

"A'ight. Be easy, man, and stay cool before you go over there and straight snap on the girl."

I jumped in my whip and jammed my foot hard down on the pedal, sending the car flying up the street. This was the craziest shit I ever heard. If any of this shit was true, it was a wrap for us, on Gawd! It took me ten minutes to get to her house. I stormed in that house looking for her ass like a bounty hunter.

"Zuri!" I yelled.

"I'm in the kitchen," she yelled back.

When I hit the corner, she was sitting at the kitchen table drinking tequila, looking all depressed and shit.

"What's going on?"

I sat across from her and took a deep breath, along with a shot of tequila. I didn't know how bad things were about to get, but I sure as hell was about to find out. Zuri knew I didn't have a Facebook, but nothing happened in the streets without me hearing about it.

"Nothing much, just waiting on you."

"How was your massage?"

"It was good."

"Did you get the hot rocks too?"

"Yeah."

"What else did you do?" My eyes were trained on her and I didn't blink once.

This was her moment of truth and I hoped she kept it a bill wit' a nigga or we was gone have some serious problems. One thing I hated was a lying-ass woman, so she better get to bumpin' her gums with some factual shit.

"I've been relaxing."

That lie slid off her tongue too quick for me and she looked me in the eyes when she said that shit. My glare was so evil and I felt like snapping her neck like a muthafuckin' Popsicle stick. I ain't have time for no bullshit ass games, so I cut straight to the chase.

"In your defense, do you have anything you want to say to me?"

Zuri was looking all confused and shit, like she didn't know what I was talking about. "What do you mean?"

"Come on, Zuri, don't play me like I'm some sucka-ass nigga."

"Bae, what are you talking about?"

I slammed my fist hard on the table and she jumped. "Why the fuck you playin' games wit' me? You better get to talkin', or this shit won't end well for you."

"Baby." She was trying to butter a nigga up with her soft voice and innocent demeanor. "Just tell me what you talkin' about. I don't have a reason to lie to you and I'm not hiding nothing from you."

"What the fuck you and Kyra was fighting for?"

Her eyes stretched wide as mine when I saw that damn video. "Yeah, spill it and stop fuckin' around. I done seen the shit on Facebook. All of Lauderdale know what's going on. Go and look before you start lying."

Zuri opened her Facebook and scrolled down her time-line. Her fingers stopped moving and they began to shake. She took a deep breath, before she started talking. "The other day we got into an argument, and she told me that she had been fucking my daddy when we were in middle school. Then, she sent me a video of her sleeping with my ex. So, when I left here today, I saw her at the store and I ran up on her."

"So, you around here fighting over a nigga you ain't fuckin'?"

"It's the principle. She tried me hard. You should've heard the shit she was saying to me. I just snapped."

"You know how that shit make me look out here? My lady out here fighting over another nigga?"

"I'm sorry."

"That ain't good enough," I reiterated, making sure she understood where I was coming from. "That shit don't sit well with me."

"I'm sorry."

"Stop saying you sorry, 'cause that don't mean shit to me right now. If I would've never said anything to you, I still wouldn't know." I rubbed my hand across my face. "So, let me ask you this." I hesitated, so I could focus on my question. "All I wanna know is, if you was fuckin' yo' daddy and wouldn't testify against him in court?"

Zuri exhaled deeply and stared at me for a hot minute. "I didn't want you to find out this way. I wanted to tell you so many times, but I was scared I would lose you."

"What the fuck does that mean?" I leaned forward in the chair. For the first time, I noticed her fear by the way she was trying to avoid the question.

"It's complicated and I was young." Zuri sighed, but not answering the question.

"You better get to un-complicating shit before I walk up out this bitch for good."

Zuri sat and played with her fingers. Then, tears escaped her eyes slowly and rolled down her cheeks.

"You just don't understand."

The softer part of me wanted to hold her in my arms and comfort her, but the gangsta in me spoke up. *"Don't let her trick you wit' them tears, nigga. These broads be lying and trying to move a nigga on emotions. Don't fall for that shit."*

Following my first mind, I sat back and waited on her to talk. "I'm listening."

Zuri went back to her childhood and told me all the things that happened between her and that punk-ass nigga that gave her life. Just listening to her go back to her younger years, made me want to throw up. As a man, I had zero understanding for molestation. They was wasting taxpayers' dollars keeping that nigga alive. Daman's ass belonged in the fryer.

After listening to this sad-ass story, I got up. This shit was too much to deal with at that time. It wasn't like she came out and told me on her own, so the confession felt different coming from her mouth. It felt forced and not voluntary. Zuri stopped talking and looked up at me.

"What's wrong?"

"I can't do this right now. I need some time to think about this and let it marinate. I'll be back when I'm ready to discuss this, but right now this is a lot for me to take in."

"You just gone leave me like this?"

"Zuri, baby. You have to understand how I feel about all of this and this is a lot to take in, and I feel like if yo' homegirl never blew the whistle, you would've never told me. Don't you think this was something that should've been discussed in the beginning?"

"We've only been together for a month. How much do you expect to learn in such a short time?" She wiped the tears from her eyes and stood up. "You didn't give me a chance to open up to you."

"I'm sorry."

I walked away from her and went to the front door. Her feet slapped hard against the tile behind me. "Please, don't leave me. I need you."

As I unlocked the front door, she tried blocking my path, but I wasn't staying under no circumstances. That was in my mind before I got there and there was no changing my mind. I wouldn't care if she cried blood.

"Zuri, move please, so I can go."

"You went through all of this to get me and you'll walk away so easily? That's not fair." Her eyes were red and her face was soaked in tears, but I turned away so I didn't have to see the pain in her eyes. As gently as possible, I moved her from the walkway and went outside. Her cries and screams shattered my heart, but I had to do what was best for me. My mind told me I didn't have the energy to love a woman like that, so I walked away for good, with no intention on coming back. Whatever I left at her place could be easily replaced.

***

One hour later, I found myself sliding on I-95, doing seventy-five in the HOV lane and jamming Jeezy's, "All There," coming back from Boca Raton.

Bout to pull up nigga make sure y'all there I just left Walters nigga I bought all pars Pull up to the spot, you might just see your dog there, Pull up unannounced you probably see your broad there, Dope jumping out the pot, like a frog yeah...

I had my Kush and Cîroc. Hell, I even popped a molly. So, yeah, I was on one. Zuri had my mind in a fucked-up place and I couldn't think straight. When I touched down, I swung by and picked up Mariah, so we could chill. Just to take my mind off of things. I didn't feel like sitting in one spot, so we rode around and sipped. We slid through a few club spots to see what was jumpin', but we didn't get out.

"So, where you been at these past few days?" Mariah popped her lips loudly.

"I was out of town," I lied. "Why, did you miss me or something?" Our eyes connected for a split second and she had this dreamy look in them.

"We never finished where we left off." Her tone was seductive and I saw right through that shit.

"Shit, we can do that now." Once again, I was single and technically, a free agent.

There was a city park on the right side of Sunrise Boulevard, so I pulled into a parking spot and backed in. In this game, I had to be on point at all times. Pushing my seat back, I let it slide all the way back and unbuckled my pants, freeing my limp pole.

Mariah knew just what to do to make it stand up. She licked the tip of it first, before nibbling softly on the head. The up and down motion was all that could be seen through my eyes. I placed my hand on her head, but I didn't choke her this time. Instead, I sat back and tried my best to enjoy it, but Zuri kept popping up in my head. Although I told her it was over, I couldn't shake her from my mind or the shit she told me. Inside my console, I remembered I had some condoms, so I reached into it and pulled one out.

"Hold up." Mariah stopped and sat upright, so I slid it over my hard wood. "Come on and ride it," I instructed her.

She climbed on top, lifted her dress and tried sliding down on my erection, but I was too big for such easy access. Mariah was a slim chick, so she was able to get on top with the limited space. Placing my hands on her shoulders, I pulled her down forcibly onto me.

"Ooh," she screamed.

I had no business hitting this young-ass chick, but mentally, I wasn't all there and I needed to release some pressure in any way possible. Mariah was moaning and biting her lip as she took the dick. Using one hand, I placed my thumb on her clit and played with it, while I dug her out. That drove her crazy. She started bouncing on it and her moans grew louder and louder. For a slim chick, she took that dick better than I thought she would. That probably came from taking plenty of dick. I squeezed down on her cheeks hard, pushing her down further into my lap. I wanted to feel her chest cavity. Car sex wasn't the best shit smoking, but I knew how to maneuver in that muthafucka. After some hard fucking for about ten minutes, I was ready to bust and drop her off. Concentrating hard on that nut, I was able to bust. When I was done, she got up and I snatched the condom off, tossing it out the window.

Once we cleaned up, I pulled off. It was late, so I was ready to drop her off and take it in for the night. The back street was dark, but after a mile, I pulled up to a red light.

A car pulled up next to me, so I looked to my right, but the tints were so dark that I couldn't see inside. Just as I was about to hit the gas, the sound of gunshots made me pause. When I realized I was wrong about the sound, it was too late, 'cause a hail of bullets came ripping through the doors, hitting the passenger side. I floored it and the only thing that could be heard was me burning rubber, trying to get away. I looked over at Mariah and she was struggling to breathe as she coughed up blood.

"Brick, it burns," she cried and held onto her chest, while she squirmed in the passenger seat.

"I know just sit tight and I'll get you to a hospital."

The nearest hospital was roughly ten minutes away, so I gunned it all the way there. If five-O hit the lights on my ass they was gone have to run it, 'cause I wasn't stopping. Mariah had become silent and I panicked.

"Mariah. Mariah. Open your eyes." I shook her body, but she was slowly fading away.

"I can't. I'm getting sleepy."

"Mariah, you gotta stay up."

Finally pulling in front of the emergency doors, I held down on the horn before getting out. Seconds later, one of the hospital staff members came out to help.

"Sir, what happened?" she asked, coming to Mariah's aid. She checked her pulse.

"We were just shot at."

"What's her name and how old is she?" she asked.

"Mariah and she's nineteen. Help her and stop asking me all these damn questions," I yelled.

"You need help too, so come on. Grab that wheelchair at the door."

I looked down at my shirt and it had blood on it, but I didn't recall being hit. My adrenaline was pumping so hard, it would be hard to tell if I had been shot. The chair was close to the door, so I ran and got it and helped her get Mariah in it. Quickly heading back to the driver's side, the nurse tried to stop me.

"Sir, where are you going?" she asked.

"I'm moving my car. I'm not going anywhere."

"Okay. Come to the back so we can check you. I'm taking her in now." The nurse pushed her through the doors fast as hell.

Snatching my shirt off, I checked to see if I had been hit, but I was good. As bad as I wanted to stay, I left the hospital to keep from being interrogated by the police. My concern was finding out who shot my shit up. I knew I had to ditch the car, because they would be looking for it tomorrow. Thank God, the shit wasn't in my name.

Chapter 19

Brick

One week later

Shit had gotten really crazy over a short period of time. I was supposed to be out here getting money, fucking ho's and living it up. Not shooting people, getting shot at, causing death or hiding out. The other night had been bothering me heavy. I was still in shock that Mariah died because of me. I wasn't sure why I was clapped up, but I was going to find out. No one saw me that night I hit up Playa, so it wasn't that and I didn't leave any evidence behind. One thing was for sure though. I wouldn't be caught slipping no more.

When I was up in Coleman, I had this one officer named Jessica that I dipped into every once in a while, she hooked me up with a going-away package. She sent a nigga a fit, some fresh jays and a cell phone. I was grateful for what she did, because she didn't have to do that. Before I got out, I told her I would look out for her on whatever she needed, so I made good on that promise. It was nothing to hit her up with a few bands and good dick during her stay. Shorty could've lost her job behind me, but she remained solid with a nigga.

Jessica hit me up, because she was going through some shit with her baby daddy. Apparently, they had broken up and she wanted to get away for a few days. We hadn't talked or seen each other in a minute, but I told her I would pay for her a flight into the West Palm Beach Airport. After I scooped her up, we went to the hotel room I got close to the airport.

We sat in the kitchen so I could roll up. "I was surprised to hear from you. Shit must've went south real quick, because the last time we spoke, you said y'all was getting married."

Jessica sighed, while resting her chin on her fist. "Yeah, that's what I thought, but we are done for good now."

"Yeah, right. I call bullshit." That's what every female said about their baby daddy.

"I'm serious."

"You just here because you mad with him and when that shit die down, you'll be right back with him." I licked the blunt and wrapped it tight.

"No, I won't."

"You say that now."

"He fucked my sister, so I will never fuck with him again in life, and I put that on my daughter."

I almost dropped my damn weed when she said that. "What? Run that by me again." That sounded crazy, so I had to hear that again.

"He fucked my sister."

"Damn, that's crazy."

"Tell me about it. They tried to apologize, but I don't have shit to say to neither one of them. Both of them bitches dead to me."

Jessica needed the weed more than I did, so I lit it and passed it to her. "Here, hit this shit. It'll take your mind off of it."

She hit the weed and we got on some alcohol. Hell, I even got her to pop a pill, so I knew shit must've been bad. We were turned up to the max. We started kissing and feeling on each other right there in the kitchen. I picked her up and placed her on the counter. Jessica was wearing a dress with no panties, so that was easy access for me. I placed my hand between her legs and rubbed on her clit until it swelled. Slowly, I dipped two fingers into her pussy, finger fucking her slowly. She was good and wet. The times we fucked when I first came home, I wasn't eating her pussy since she was back fucking her baby daddy. And, I still wasn't doing it. The only pussy I was eating was Zuri's. I missed her so much, but I couldn't have a conversation with her over the phone. The things I wanted to say to her had to be said in person. We weren't together, so technically, I wasn't cheating.

One thing I knew about her was that she loved this shit. Every time we locked down, she made it her business to pull me out my cell, so I could drop this rod off in her. I dropped my pants and rammed in every inch, until she swallowed me whole.

"Mmm. Shit." Jessica gasped for air and wrapped her legs around my waist and grinded with me. "Yes, Zaddy. Yes. Just like that."

I was sucking on her neck, making sure I left marks on her bright skin behind, just in case she was lying. The mention of the name *Zaddy* made Zuri pop into my head, causing me to pause mid-stroke. That was what she called me and now I felt somewhat bad for what I was doing. But it was too late because I had flown Jessica here out of anger. Once she left, I had to go and make things right between us. Zuri deserve that treatment and I should've never treated her like some random bitch I was fuckin' with. I really cared about her, but the shit I heard was downright disturbing. Maybe I should've stayed and worked through the problem. Once I was back in her good graces, I was going to do right by her and get a better understanding of what she went through.

Jessica was grinding against me and pulling me by my waist trying to get my attention. "Why did you stop?"

"Hold on." Rubbing my hand over my face, I sighed. I had to shake Zuri from my head.

"Beat this pussy," she whispered in my ear.

Pulling her closer to the edge, I held her hips and beat her down just the way she like it.

"Ah. Ah. Fuck. Me. Ooh," she begged.

That lasted for a few minutes and right before I was about to cum, she hopped off the counter and got down on her knees. Face-to-face with my rod, she slurped it into her mouth and worked those throat muscles like a pro. I threw my head back and held onto the counter. Her head game was so strong, she made my damn knees buckle. My dick exploded without warning. In the middle of it, I grabbed her hair and snatched her head back, so I could bust all over her lips. We took the next several rounds to the bedroom and fucked each other for hours, before we finally fell asleep.

***

Four days later, we were still confined to the room, but it was her last day. Me and Jessica got down like rabbits the whole time she was there. She stepped from the bathroom, fully dressed.

"I'm ready."

"Damn, I thought you were coming out in a towel or some shit."

"My flight leaves in an hour and we don't have time for a quickie." She walked up to me and kissed me in the mouth. "We spent the past few days on top of each other, you're not tired?"

"I don't get tired." I laughed. "My stamina too high for that. Five years a long time to go without pussy. I'm trying to catch up."

"I bet you don't, but I'll be back."

"I know you will."

During the ride to the airport, we didn't talk. I was too busy jamming Kevin Gates', "I Don't Get Tired." I looked over at her and rapped a few lines to her.

"Six weeks ago I just purchased a foreign, Most likely the one that you cannot afford, Right foot on the gas Balenciaga be accelerating, I'm doing the dash, Chick that I'm with, Shorty be doing her shit. And it's okay to say that she bad, Look to the right and I give her a glance, Pray to God we don't, pray to God we don't crash. I was trying to get it how I live, I want them dead presidents, I want to pull up, head spent, get it, get fly I got six jobs I don't get tired."

Five minutes later, I pulled up in front of the terminal and helped her with her bags. She looked at me and smiled.

"I really enjoyed our time together and I hope this won't be the last time."

Being the man I am, I stepped up closer and gave her a hug, while grabbing a handful of ass in the process.

"It won't be, so don't worry and I had a good time too. Have a safe flight."

"I'll text you when I land."

"A'ight."

***

It was time I graced Broward County with my presence. I had been ducked off for a week and it was time to bleed the block. Whatever happened was gone transpire and I was locked and loaded for whatever was coming my way. Once I was smooth sailing on I-95 North, I hit up Skeet.

"What up, boss? Wae ya at wit' it?" He picked up.

"I'm headed back to Broward. What's going on?"

"It's some funny shit goin' on and I just wanted to put you up on game."

"What's that, youngin'?" I turned off the stereo so I didn't miss a beat.

"That nigga, Gucci, stepped down from his position and gave it to that nigga, Mel. Y'all family and shit, so why not pass you that clientele?"

My jaw clenched up tight from hearing the bullshit, but I knew better than to jump to conclusions. In my meeting, I clearly stated that he needed to choose wisely, so for his sake this better be a misunderstanding. I needed to holla at the nigga myself, so I could see where his head was at. For all I knew, he could be getting high with the flakka-head chick he wore on his arm, like that ho' was the Queen of England or some shit.

"A'ight, fam, good looking. I'ma check that shit out when I hit the block. Get the crew together for a meeting in the morning at ten."

"Gotcha, boss," Skeet replied.

"Keep ya ear to the streets and good work. I see you workin' and that shit ain't going unnoticed. Keep doin' ya thang and I promise it gets greater later."

"I 'preciate that, boss."

"Tomorrow." Then, I hung up the phone.

Once again, my head was on a swivel, but I had one more situation to handle. Gucci would be seeing me soon and I put that on my dead mama. Mark my muthafuckin' words. When I got off on Sunrise, I swung by the flower shop on the corner to place an order. Some young chick was working at the register.

"Good afternoon. How can I help you?" I looked at her name tag and smiled.

"Hey Maria, let me get a dozen of red roses." I reached into my pocket and pulled out a knot of money. Her eyes never left my hand, as I counted off thirteen one-hundred-dollar bills and handed them to her.

Maria laughed. "They don't cost that much."

"Yeah, I know. I want you to wrap each one of these bills around every flower. That's thirteen hundred dollars, so you can keep the change."

"Thank you. Have a seat and I'll get this done right now."

"You're welcome."

***

It only took twenty minutes for her to get my special order together. Zuri's car was in the driveway when I pulled up, so I used the key to gain entrance. I knew one muthafuckin' thang, her ass better not have company or somebody was going to the morgue today and it wasn't me. When I walked in the room, she was sitting on the bed staring down at her hands. There was music playing loudly, so I knew she didn't know that I came in.

Baby, I know what you've been through
So I'm here to relieve you, remind you, renew you
rebuild you, girl, I'll do whatever it takes just to reshape
what he mess up, cause real love needs real love
And I'm here love cause I need you.

Oh, and taking me away from you will be no damn good for me, I need you in my life, No one could compare to you.

Keyshia Cole's lyrics to "Losin' You" spoke to me. Therefore, I knew what she was going though and it was all because of my inability to be sensitive towards her.

"Baby," I called out, startling her. Zuri looked up at me with bright red eyes and a tear-stained face, but she remained silent. "What's wrong?"

Taking slow strides towards her, I proceeded with caution. As I got closer, whatever she had in her hands she clutched it tightly, so I couldn't see it. I handed her the flowers and she took a quick glance at them, before tossing them beside her.

"You don't like the flowers?" It was a silly question, but I needed her to talk to me.

"Thank you, but I don't want them." She sniffled.

"Zuri, I know you mad at me, but I came to apologize. I've thought about you every day and I can't be without you."

"That sounds a lot like your last speech. Did you practice that on the way here or did you know it by heart?"

"No. I'm telling you how I really feel. This is new to me and I'm not the sensitive type, so please forgive me for the way I acted last week."

Zuri nodded her head up and down. "The roses." She paused, then dropped her head. "That's your peace offering? 'Cause I can't be bought."

Gently, I placed my finger underneath her chin and raised her head, so I could look in her eyes. "Come on beautiful. You know that's not what I'm trying to do."

"Then what are you trying to do? Kick me when I'm down? Make me feel like I'm less of a woman because of

196

my past or make me feel guilty, based on the decisions I made? Which one is it, Brandon?"

"No. I would never do that to you and I handled that all wrong. I just didn't know how to respond. I've never been in a situation like this before."

Zuri stared vacantly into my remorseful eyes. "So, the best thing for you to do was leave me here alone to battle with my issues and feelings about you? That wasn't fair and you know it."

"You're right and I fucked up. I'm man enough to admit that. All I want is another chance to prove to you that I'm a good man and I can be all you need."

"Don't you think it's a little too late for that?"

"It's never too late for love. Just let me love you past your pain."

"How can I be sure that you won't give up on me and leave once again?"

The brittle sound of her voice pierced my heart. My glassy eyes matched hers and I felt a deeper connection to her than I did last week. I had to commend Zuri on her strength to live her life. Many women aren't successful once they've become victims of sexual abuse. Sometimes, they end up fucked up and on drugs, but she worked as a counselor to help those same kids.

I grabbed her free hand and kneeled down, clutching it tight before kissing it.

"Listen, baby, from the bottom of my heart, I'm sorry and I should've never walked out the way I did. That shit was a lot to take in and I reacted on impulse."

She listened attentively.

"You have to understand that I'm not easily moved on emotion, so that won't work on me. I'm hard in relationships, but I take care of home first. You will always be my priority and I will always focus on making you happy, to the best of my ability. I hate a liar and I don't like hearing shit in the streets about my woman."

Zuri was awfully emotional, as the tears constantly flooded down her face and onto my arms. There was something deeper bothering her and I needed to get to the bottom of it. I grabbed her other hand, but she snatched it away from me.

"What's in your hand that you don't want me to see?" She froze when I mentioned it, so I held my hand out. "Let me see it."

Zuri dropped a white stick in my hand. The first thing I noticed were two pink lines. I wasn't a dummy, so I knew exactly what I was looking at.

"You pregnant?"

She seemed afraid to answer, so she waited for a few seconds before nodding her head. "Yes."

"So, that's why you keep crying?"

"Yes." She wiped her face with the sleeve of her long-sleeved shirt.

"Why? It's not the end of the world."

"You not mad?"

"Why would I be mad? This was bound to happen." I stood back on my feet.

"I don't know. I guess 'cause it's still early and I didn't know if you wanted kids or not." Her voice was so soft and innocent.

"I'm a grown-ass man. If I didn't want kids, I would strap up with you, but I know you will be a great mother."

"Are you happy?"

"Zuri, I love you. Of course I'm happy, but let me show you how happy I am. Get dressed."

"Where are we going?"

"It's a surprise."

"Okay."

Zuri got up and went into the bathroom to get ready for what I had in store for her. She had no idea this was the best news I heard all day and for that, she would be rewarded.

Chapter 20

Gucci

For the past week, I been ducked off in Fort Myers, getting myself together. I purchased a four-bedroom house and I just closed on it. Mehzani and I would be moving in soon. My plan to leave the streets had been signed, sealed and delivered. Mel had officially taken over and I would have no further dealings with the dope game. Brick was gone be mad when he found out, but he would be okay. I delivered on my promise to link him with the distributor and now he was on his own. Now, it was up to him to flood the streets and create his own clientele.

This was the best decision I'd made in my life. The only thing left to do was take my mom out of the rehab center. I looked into getting her some private care, so she wouldn't be in a home. My schedule would now permit me to spend more time with her and take care of her needs as well. I had long-term plans for Mehzani. She didn't know about the house, so it was going to be a surprise, along with the proposal. Before I left Lauderdale for good, I had a few loose ends to tie up. I locked up the house and got back on the road.

My phone vibrated in my pocket. I took it out and the name *Shark* lit up, so I answered it.

"Hello."

"Where you at?" Shark asked, with a bit of attitude.

"I'm headed to you, what's up?"

"Nothing. I'm just making sure you didn't forget about me, that's all."

I laughed. "Nah. You ain't gone let me do that and I told you I had some important business to finish."

"Well, I'm here waiting."

"Okay, I'll be there."

"Yeah."

***

After driving for two hours, I made it back safely to Broward County. My first stop was the Marriott in Weston. I went up to the fourth floor and knocked on the door. About forty seconds later, it opened and Shark stepped to the side to let me in.

"About time. It only took you forever to get here. I swear, you can't tell time," Shark complained, while closing the door behind us.

Leading the way, I followed her into the living room part of the suite. This heffa was crazy and I called her Shark, because she was a predator and for the life of me, I couldn't understand how I got involved with her in the first place.

"I had some business to take care of, but I told you I was coming. Damn, quit complaining all the time. That's why you single now."

That muthafucka rolled her eyes hard and I just knew they were gone get stuck. "Yeah, you did, but you know I get impatient and besides, I made special arrangements to be here overnight. I had to pay my mama to babysit. You know how she is."

"I do." I rubbed my hands on my jeans. "So, what's going on?"

"Shit, everything but right now, I don't want to talk about that just yet. I can't focus properly until I'm relaxed. I need a fix and I've been waiting."

Shark caressed my chest underneath my shirt, making a slow trail to my belly button and inside my boxers. My dick jumped at her touch. She unbuckled my belt, then my pants before freeing my soldier. He was slowly rising to attention, when she wrapped her lips around his neck and stroked it.

"Ooh, shit." Using my left hand, I played in her hair and put my phone on silent with the other. "Argh," I grunted.

Her lips massaged my head, as she rocked the mic. "Suck that shit," I whispered, while rubbing her head. She was wearing a wig, so I couldn't feel her scalp. Females got on my nerves wearing all that bullshit. Whenever I get some sloppy toppy, I need to be able to massage that scalp.

Those skills were exactly how it all started between me and her a few years back. We were never in a relationship. It was supposed to be a one-time thing, but when her nigga went to jail, I stepped in and helped her out. In return, she would bust it open for a nigga. When she made the offer, I declined on several occasions. Then, one day when I came over, she was wearing some boy shorts, exposing her pussy print and it was on from then. All we did was smoke and fuck. I never took her out and we always tried to remain discreet about it. A few nosey muthafuckas were trying to dig, but they kept coming up empty every time. My plan was to go to the grave with this secret.

"Mount up," I demanded.

Removing my pants, I kicked them off to the side. Shark straddled me and lowered herself down slowly, until I was deep inside. Slowly, she rocked back and forth, with her eyes closed.

"Play with that pussy." She followed my instructions and placed her fingers on her clit. Her fingers moved back and forth on it, while I caressed her breasts with both hands.

"Ahh." Her eyes were clamped down shut and her mouth was agape. I could see the back of her throat.

Using two fingers, I rubbed her clit, soaking them with her own juices and stuck my fingers in her mouth. Shark sucked down on them like she had my dick in her mouth. Her pussy muscles had a death grip on my shit when she bounced up and down on it. My hands were tight on her waist and our thrusts matched blow for blow. We were both sweating like dogs in the cold room.

"I'm finna cum." She bit her lip and rubbed her clit faster. I was right behind her when I felt it pulsate against her walls. My stomach muscles tightened when I started to let loose.

"Shit. Shit." Each thrust was more aggressive than the last one, as I rocked her hard against my pelvis. The eruption finally occurred and I was winded like a muthafucka, but she was still moving.

"Unh-unh, be still." Her thighs were vibrating and she started to slow down.

"Ah. Ah. Ss." All movement came to a complete stop and she collapsed on top of me, burying her head in the side of my neck. "Damn."

We stayed that way for a few minutes before she finally broke our silence. "What are we gonna do about our situation?"

"What?" I played dumb, knowing damn well what she was talking about.

"The situation with Brick." She took a deep breath. "As much as I can't stand his ass, he deserves to know. This has been going on for too long now."

I sighed long and hard. "I don't know. I'll figure something out soon."

She sat up quick and frowned. "What you mean soon? This was supposed to been handled."

"Deja, what the fuck do you expect me to say? Stop being so fuckin' impatient."

"Make me think you scared of his ass too," Deja snapped.

"Get up, man. I ain't on this shit. I have enough shit going on already and I don't need no additional headaches." It was time for me to clear it and take my ass home. My ass should've never came here in the first place." I snatched my clothes up and got dressed.

"Where are you going?" She folded her arms across her chest and rocked on her heels.

"I'm going home. I don't know who you think you talking to, but you got me fucked up if you think I'm scared of the nigga."

"I can't tell, you let that nigga spit in my face." Deja's mouth could be reckless and that was why Brick pulled that stunt at the liquor store. Her ass talked too fuckin' much. That bitch never knew when to shut up, except when a dick was in her damn mouth. After tonight, she was on her own with all her drama. In the next few weeks, I was gone be out of Broward for good and wouldn't have to deal with none of this shit. I hope she enjoyed the dick, because that was the very last time she would feel this again.

A week ago, I ran into that nigga on a late night and I let the heat go on his ass. I sprayed his car until the clip was empty. He was slipping and I lucked up on the bust, but it wasn't successful. The nigga was still breathing.

The streets were talking about the incident and that was how I found out about the end result. That shit threw me,

Destiny Skai

because I put over a dozen bullets in that nigga's shit. I also heard one of his boys was out there, trying to get info on the shooting, so I knew I needed to stay strapped and walk light. There were some stories about him in a span of a few weeks, but I already knew he was a force to be reckoned with. That didn't deter me from my mission, because I didn't fear any man that bled red blood just like me, but he wasn't about to catch me off guard. That nigga was swift and he moved like a ninja 'round this bitch.

This time, I was bringing that real firepower. I was gonna light up the city like the muthafuckin' Fourth of July. Target practice was over and this time around, I was hitting every major artery. So, that nigga better wear his bullet-proof vest all muthafuckin' day long. It was guaranteed the next time I clapped at his ass, I was gone send him to his final resting place and that would be very soon. Before I left for Fort Myers, God was my witness. Brick was gone be buried beside his mother in a deep dark ditch. *So, let the muthafuckin' murder games begin.*

206

Chapter 21

Brick

The sounds of giggling and water splashing made me happy being a father. Just seeing the huge smile on my baby girl's face was priceless. I swear the best things in life were free.

"Daddy, can you wash my hair? I don't like when Mommy do it."

"Sure thing, princess. Yo' mama do it too rough?"

Breanna nodded her head up and down. "Yeah."

I looked down at her with my brow bent. "What was that?"

"I mean yes."

"That's better." Respect was the most important concept she needed to learn in life and I was going to make sure I embedded that into her tiny brain by any means necessary at a young age.

"Deja." I screamed.

"Yeah." Her voice was low so I knew she was close by. When I turned around she was leaning against the door with her arms folded.

"Where's the shampoo?"

"Under the sink." Deja bent down and took the bottle from the cabinet and handed it to me. "You know she missed you terribly while you were away."

Quickly taking it from her hand and blatantly ignoring her comment, I turned my attention back to my daughter. She didn't need to tell me shit because it was her fault my baby couldn't see me while I was away. Stank ass ho'.

"You ready?"

"Yes."

Once I removed the ponytail holder from her thick, curly hair it fell down immediately and bounced. She definitely had my good grade of hair because her mammy shit was nappy as fuck. Thank God for the little miracles in life. I squeezed some shampoo into my hand and placed the bottle on the side of the tub. Then I applied it thoroughly to her hair, making sure I tackled every inch.

"Keep your eyes closed, baby."

Breanna squeezed them together as tight as her eyelids allowed, exposing her cheekbones and dimple. I loved my baby beyond the earth, moon and stars, and there was nothing I wouldn't do for her. I'll bury a nigga and bitch about mine. Those years away from her did a number on me and I vowed to never leave her again. As I massaged her scalp a few suds splashed on my pants.

"Alright let's rinse this out, but keep your eyes closed. You doing a good job, baby."

Breanna knew the routine as she slid closer to the spigot and tilted her head back. I washed the suds from her hair and gave her a bath before taking her out the tub with her princess towel. On the way to her bedroom my phone started ringing, so I sat her down on the bed to see who was calling. It was Skeet.

"Whaddup?"

"Aye, man, I'm at the car show at the park on Sunrise and it's time to take out the trash. Ya' boy out here flossin'. We need to handle that shit before the party."

"A'ight. I'll be there soon. Hit me up if the location changes."

"Gotcha."

I hung up with Skeet and hit up Coop.

"What's up, bruh?"

"Aye, nigga, it's show time. Come scoop me up from Deja house."

"Fuck you doin' over there?" Coop sounded shocked.

"It ain't what you thinkin', bruh. I'm on daddy duty."

"Better be."

"Come on, man, that shit been dead and you know that. You know I wouldn't…" I paused, remembering that my baby was right there listening.

"Ooh Daddy, you said a curse word." Breanna had her hand over her mouth.

"I gotta go, man. Hurry up."

"I'm close, so I'll be there in fifteen minutes."

"Yeah." I hung the phone up and tossed it on the bed. "Come on let's get you dressed."

On limited time now, I had to hurry up and get Breanna situated. I passed her a pair of panties and a pajama set. When she was fully dressed, I brushed her hair into a ponytail and put a scarf on it. It wasn't perfect, but it would do for bedtime. Breanna jumped into bed and waited on me to tuck her in.

"Daddy, can you read me Princess and the Frog?" she exclaimed with so much happiness in her voice.

Normally I would let her pick whatever story she wanted to hear, but tonight was different. I was headed out to do dirt and I had no idea how any of this shit was going to play out. It was risky running down on this nigga in public and out in the open, but I didn't have a choice. It was now or never. Legend was a hard muthafucka to catch, so I had to take the opportunity and be discreet as possible.

"Not tonight, baby. Daddy will read that to you tomorrow. We're going to do something different okay?"

"Okay."

"Here get down on the floor with me and get on your knees." Breanna followed my instructions and kneeled down beside me. With her small hand in mine I took a deep breath and looked over at her.

"Close your eyes."

The second she closed them I began.

"The Lord is my Shepherd, I shall not want, He maketh me to lie down in green pastures: He leadeth me beside the still waters. He restoreth my soul: He leadeth me in the paths of righteousness for His name sake."

A huge lump formed in my throat and I could feel myself choking up. Just the thought of never seeing Breanna's face again was fucking with me heavy. Out of all the shit I did since I've been home not once had I felt this way. I didn't know if it was God telling me to sit this one out or what. All I knew was that something didn't feel right. Pulling myself together, I finished up.

"Yea, though I walk through the valley of the shadow of death, I will fear no evil: For thou art with me. Thy rod and thy staff, they comfort me. Thou preparest a table before me in the presence of mine enemies; Thou annointest my head with oil; surely, mercy and goodness shall follow me all the days of my life and I will dwell in the house of the Lord forever. Amen."

"Amen." Breanna repeated.

When I looked up, she was staring me in the face. Her faced was balled up. "What's wrong, Daddy?"

"Nothing, baby. I'm okay." I lied.

She wiped my eyes. "Then why are you crying?"

I rubbed my hand over face to play it off. "Daddy got something in his eyes. Come on let's get you into bed."

Breanna got back into bed and I tucked her in. Coop was outside because my phone was going off once again. I picked the phone up, but I didn't answer it. Instead I leaned down and kissed Breanna on her lips.

"I love you, princess, and I'll see you tomorrow."

"You promise?"

"I promise. Cross my heart and hope to die." I drew an invisible cross over my chest.

"I love you, too, Daddy."

"Goodnight." I walked away with the weight of the world on my shoulders. Whatever happened tonight I knew I needed to be extra careful. I couldn't afford any slip-ups like the first-time 'cause there wasn't going to be another Zuri to save me.

***

The car show was thick as fuck, so by the time we got there they weren't letting anybody else inside the park. We had to swap cars and that took up more time.

"Ain't that a bitch?" Coop said.

"It's all good we can't do shit in there anyway. That shit too muthafuckin' crowded. A nigga will be handcuffs and booked in the county jail or in a body bag for busting off in that bitch."

"Facts, bruh. Straight muthafuckin' facts."

"I'm 'bouta hit Skeet up and see what the play is." I grabbed my phone and hit him up.

"Yo."

"Aye, man, we can't get in that shit." I looked around and these niggas was straight clowning in traffic.

"Go over to Lauderhill Mall and sit in the parking lot. We headed out now."

"A'ight."

"Slide over to the mall. Them niggas going across the street."

It took us ten minutes to bust a U-turn to get up out that bitch and another ten to get in the parking lot at the mall. One of the niggas who slid up on me the other day when I was in the city was posted up in a Cadillac truck on twenty-six-inch rims, blasting music. My ass was incognito so I wasn't about to show my face. I ain't trust none of these snitchin' ass niggas. The only one I trusted was in the driver seat. We were backed in so we can smash some shit and clear it. A text message came through and Zuri came to mind, but when I looked down it was Skeet. He sent me a photo of the car to look for.

Brick: Delete that shit out your phone. Pics and the thread. Hit me up in the am.

Skeet: Ok

After sitting in the car for another thirty minutes the Teal Vert Skeet sent me came through bumping some loud ass music. The only problem was he was one row away and he was backing in as well.

"That's the nigga right there," I said to Coop.

"How you wanna get this nigga?"

"We gotta get close to his ass. We gon' wait for him to step out the car and I'm blasting his ass after that."

"A'ight."

We sat and stalked our prey like some vultures. All I needed was his ass to get out his car and post up. Not even five minutes later I saw him get out from the driver seat.

"Hit it, bruh."

"I see him." Coop pulled out and went left so he could be on my side.

The parking lot was thick too, but everybody seemed drunk and in a zone. I pulled the AK-47 from the backseat and made sure my bitch was ready to let loose.

"Slide slow, but don't stop for shit."

"Nigga, I ain't new to this shit."

"Just making sho' in case yo' ass got rusty while I was gone."

I was locked and loaded. As soon as we were one car away I held it to the window in his direction. "Hit the window."

The passenger window slid down automatically and I pointed that muthafucka toward Legend. By the time he saw what was coming, it was too late cause I was lighting that bitch up like New Year's Eve.

Frrrrrrraaaaakkkkkk!

The sound of the explosion caused an uproar to the ones near him, as they ducked down for cover. Each bullet I sent in his direction tore into his chest leaving multiple holes followed by bright red blood stains. Everything seemed like it was going in slow motion, as I watched Legend's body fall backwards and hit the pavement.

Suddenly, a familiar sound filled my ears and it was Déjà vu all over again. When I looked behind me I could see bright flashes followed by bullets slamming hard against the car.

Coop was a pro so I didn't need to tell him what to do. He hit the gas hard and got us the fuck outta there with the quickness. The second we were out of dodge I closed my eyes for a brief second and Breanna's cute face flashed before me.

We hit it straight down Sunrise Boulevard until we were able to cut through the Dillard Park neighborhood and take several back streets to safety. The car was hot so we went to drop it back off at the warehouse. Coop hit 21st Street, pulled into the storage and punched in the code. The gate opened slowly, but once we got in I knew we were home free.

During the ride back to Zuri's house, so much shit was running through my mind. The night could've really played out differently, but my boy was on point. All I wanted to do was get in the house, shower and cuddle with my lady after I took a swim in the lady lake.

Coop pulled up in the driveway. "Hit me up in the morning when you get up."

"Fa 'sho." I dapped him up and got out the car. He waited until I got inside before he pulled off.

The lights were still on so that meant she was waiting up for me. It didn't matter if she was sleep or not because I was gone get some ass regardless. Shit, I needed to let loose a few rounds. The closer I got to the room I could hear noises. Zuri didn't acknowledge my presence at all. I guess she was too caught up in whatever she was looking at in her phone.

"Bae." I called out and removed my shoes. "Come take a shower with me."

Zuri didn't open her mouth.

I took off my shirt and pants and kicked them off toward the foot of the bed. She was still in her own world, so I walked up on her. Gently I placed my hand on her shoulder.

"Zuri. You hear me talking to you?"

She looked up and her eyes were bloodshot red. That caught me off guard, especially since I wasn't expecting any of that.

"Why are you crying? What happened?" I was genuinely concerned.

"M—my." That was all she managed to say before she started wailing loudly.

It broke my heart to see her in bad shape, but I couldn't help her if I didn't know what was going on. So, I rubbed her back and tried to get her to calm down.

"Baby, I can't help you if I don't know what's going." I tilted her head up, so she could look at me. "What's going on? Why are you so upset?"

"They killed him." She sobbed.

My first thought was that someone in prison killed her punk ass daddy and if that was the case her ass should've been happy. He was the one that ruined her life in the first place.

"They killed who, baby?" Zuri kept crying and couldn't get a word out. Her chest heaved up and down like she was hyperventilating. "Zuri, baby, I can't comfort you properly if I don't what's going on." I sat down on the bed and took her in my arms. She buried her head deep in my chest. "I'm here, baby, but you gotta talk to me. Who did they kill?"

"My brother."

Now I was utterly confused because I wasn't aware that my woman even had a brother. I guess we hadn't got that far in our relationship either since I hadn't met him yet, but it was too late for that now.

"I didn't know you had a brother, but I'm sorry to hear that." I kissed her on the top of her head while continuing to comfort my world during her time of need. "I'll be here for you through it all. Whatever you need me to do, I'll do it?"

"I just want to get that image out my head." Zuri started wailing from her gut and it was the most painful sound that I'd heard in a while. That shit broke my heart in a million pieces.

"They shot my brother and while he was dying they was recording him instead of calling for fucking help. He all over social media. That's fucked up because Legend didn't do anything to anybody and they murdered my brother in cold blood like he was a fucking dog in the streets."

For clarification purposes I needed her to repeat what she just said just in case my ears weren't working properly from the sound of the gunshots. "What's his name?"

"Legend."

My entire heart hit the floor when she repeated his name and it felt like I couldn't breathe. This was unbelievable that I was the one responsible for killing my woman's brother. The more she cried, the more my heart shattered. I did that. My actions took away her loved one and now that was something I had to deal with. Coop wasn't gone believe this shit here. *How could I confess this to her?* Zuri would never forgive me for pulling that trigger, but I couldn't lie to her either. This shit was all wrong and overwhelming. My heart was thumping hard like some subwoofers. Her head was still buried in my chest, so I eased her up and kissed her passionately.

Finally letting go, I looked in her fire red eyes with so much pain and regret. "Come on let's talk about this."

To Be Continued...
Corrupted by a Gangsta 2
Coming Soon

Submission Guideline.

Submit the first three chapters of your completed manuscript to ldpsubmissions@gmail.com, subject line: Your book's title. The manuscript must be in a .doc file and sent as an attachment. Document should be in Times New Roman, double spaced and in size 12 font. Also, provide your synopsis and full contact information. If sending multiple submissions, they must each be in a separate email.

Have a story but no way to send it electronically? You can still submit to LDP/Ca$h Presents. Send in the first three chapters, written or typed, of your completed manuscript to:

LDP: Submissions Dept
Po Box 870494
Mesquite, Tx 75187

DO NOT send original manuscript. Must be a duplicate.

Provide your synopsis and a cover letter containing your full contact information.

Thanks for considering LDP and Ca$h Presents.

Destiny Skai

Coming Soon from Lock Down Publications/Ca$h Presents

BOW DOWN TO MY GANGSTA

By **Ca$h**

TORN BETWEEN TWO

By **Coffee**

BLOOD STAINS OF A SHOTTA **III**

By **Jamaica**

WHEN THE STREETS CLAP BACK **III**

By **Jibril Williams**

STEADY MOBBIN

By **Marcellus Allen**

BLOOD OF A BOSS **V**

By **Askari**

LOYAL TO THE GAME **IV**

By **T.J. & Jelissa**

A DOPEBOY'S PRAYER **II**

By **Eddie "Wolf" Lee**

IF LOVING YOU IS WRONG… **III**

LOVE ME EVEN WHEN IT HURTS

By **Jelissa**

DAUGHTERS OF A SAVAGE **II**

By **Chris Green**

SKI MASK CARTEL **III**

By **T.J. Edwards**

TRAPHOUSE KING **II**

By **Hood Rich**

218

BLAST FOR ME **II**

RAISED AS A GOON **V**

By **Ghost**

ADDICTIED TO THE DRAMA **III**

By **Jamila Mathis**

LIPSTICK KILLAH **II**

By **Mimi**

WHAT BAD BITCHES DO **2**

By **Aryanna**

THE COST OF LOYALTY **II**

By **Kweli**

SHE FELL IN LOVE WITH A REAL ONE

By **Tamara Butler**

LOVE SHOULDN'T HURT

By **Meesha**

CORRUPTED BY A GANGSTA II

By **Destiny Skai**

Available Now

RESTRAINING ORDER **I & II**

By **CA$H & Coffee**

LOVE KNOWS NO BOUNDARIES **I II & III**

By **Coffee**

RAISED AS A GOON I, II, III & IV

BRED BY THE SLUMS I, II, III

BLAST FOR ME

By **Ghost**

LAY IT DOWN **I & II**

LAST OF A DYING BREED

BLOOD STAINS OF A SHOTTA I & II

By **Jamaica**

LOYAL TO THE GAME

LOYAL TO THE GAME II

LOYAL TO THE GAME III

By **TJ & Jelissa**

BLOODY COMMAS I & II

SKI MASK CARTEL I & II

By **T.J. Edwards**

IF LOVING HIM IS WRONG…I & II

By **Jelissa**

WHEN THE STREETS CLAP BACK I & II

By **Jibril Williams**

A DISTINGUISHED THUG STOLE MY HEART I II & III

By **Meesha**

PUSH IT TO THE LIMIT

By **Bre' Hayes**

BLOOD OF A BOSS **I, II, III & IV**

By **Askari**

THE STREETS BLEED MURDER **I, II & III**

THE HEART OF A GANGSTA I II& III

By **Jerry Jackson**

CUM FOR ME

CUM FOR ME 2

CUM FOR ME 3

Corrupted by a Gangsta

An **LDP Erotica Collaboration**
BRIDE OF A HUSTLA **I II& III**
THE FETTI GIRLS **I, II& III**
CORRUPTED BY A GANGSTA
By **Destiny Skai**
WHEN A GOOD GIRL GOES BAD
By **Adrienne**
A GANGSTER'S REVENGE **I II III & IV**
THE BOSS MAN'S DAUGHTERS
THE BOSS MAN'S DAUGHTERS II
THE BOSSMAN'S DAUGHTERS III
THE BOSSMAN'S DAUGHTERS IV
A SAVAGE LOVE **I & II**
BAE BELONGS TO ME
A HUSTLER'S DECEIT I, II
By **Aryanna**
A KINGPIN'S AMBITON
A KINGPIN'S AMBITION **II**
I MURDER FOR THE DOUGH
By **Ambitious**
TRUE SAVAGE
TRUE SAVAGE II
TRUE SAVAGE **III**
DAUGHTERS OF A SAVAGE
By **Chris Green**
A DOPEBOY'S PRAYER
By **Eddie "Wolf" Lee**

221

Destiny Skai

THE KING CARTEL **I, II & III**

By **Frank Gresham**

THESE NIGGAS AIN'T LOYAL **I, II & III**

By **Nikki Tee**

GANGSTA SHYT **I II &III**

By **CATO**

THE ULTIMATE BETRAYAL

By **Phoenix**

BOSS'N UP **I , II & III**

By **Royal Nicole**

I LOVE YOU TO DEATH

By Destiny J

I RIDE FOR MY HITTA

I STILL RIDE FOR MY HITTA

By **Misty Holt**

LOVE & CHASIN' PAPER

By **Qay Crockett**

TO DIE IN VAIN

By **ASAD**

BROOKLYN HUSTLAZ

By **Boogsy Morina**

BROOKLYN ON LOCK I & II

By **Sonovia**

GANGSTA CITY

By **Teddy Duke**

A DRUG KING AND HIS DIAMOND I & II

A DOPEMAN'S RICHES

Corrupted by a Gangsta

By Nicole Goosby

TRAPHOUSE KING

By **Hood Rich**

<u>BOOKS BY LDP'S CEO, CA$H</u>

<u>TRUST IN NO MAN</u>

<u>TRUST IN NO MAN 2</u>

<u>TRUST IN NO MAN 3</u>

<u>BONDED BY BLOOD</u>

<u>SHORTY GOT A THUG</u>

<u>THUGS CRY</u>

<u>THUGS CRY 2</u>

<u>THUGS CRY 3</u>

<u>TRUST NO BITCH</u>

<u>TRUST NO BITCH 2</u>

<u>TRUST NO BITCH 3</u>

<u>TIL MY CASKET DROPS</u>

<u>RESTRAINING ORDER</u>

<u>RESTRAINING ORDER 2</u>

<u>IN LOVE WITH A CONVICT</u>

<u>Coming Soon</u>

BONDED BY BLOOD 2

BOW DOWN TO MY GANGSTA

Corrupted by a Gangsta

www.ingramcontent.com/pod-product-compliance
Lightning Source LLC
Chambersburg PA
CBHW071331250626
47159CB00004B/1551